SILVEROO

Daco Ward is a drifter with just seventy cents when Bill Dodds offers him a job. But Dodds easily makes enemies. He bests Tucker Lankton at cards and Lankton, backed by his sidekick Ed Crants, vows to get even. Daco also felt that Dodds had made a fool of him. He had a score to settle. Now Daco would find himself in the middle of a deadly game of deceit and murder, the prize being the riches of Silveroo.

JOSEPH JOHN McGRAW

SILVEROO

Complete and Unabridged

LINFORD
Leicester

First published in Great Britain in 2008 by
Robert Hale Limited
London

First Linford Edition
published 2009
by arrangement with
Robert Hale Limited
London

British Library CIP Data

McGraw, Joseph John.
    Silveroo - - (Linford western library)
    1. Western stories.
    2. Large type books.
    I. Title II. Series
    823.9'2–dc22

ISBN 978–1–84782–814–9

Published by
F. A. Thorpe (Publishing)
Anstey, Leicestershire

Set by Words & Graphics Ltd.
Anstey, Leicestershire
Printed and bound in Great Britain by
T. J. International Ltd., Padstow, Cornwall

This book is printed on acid-free paper

1

A Game of Cards

Payday in Clayton Creek, Box Tree County, was much the same as payday in any other place where men worked hard. Except they played harder there.

Clayton had been a railhead, the end of a line that began way back east. But it was so no more. Railroads were pushing west fast and towns appeared, grew and died or were left behind by the double lines of shining steel that snaked relentlessly like living tendrils across the plains. Clayton had fared better than most railheads. It had survived. The tracks going east to west happened to cross an old cattle trail running north and south. The loco sheds, smithies and repair shops had not moved on but had stayed put and grown bigger and a freight depot had sprung up alongside the fenced off pens and barns set aside for the herds that went on being driven through, as they had been for years. What had started as a settlement of tents grew into a town with regular buildings, a church, a bank, stores and sidewalks. Clayton even boasted a school. Boasted was the right word, for the townsfolk were proud of it. A town that had no school had no future. A schoolhouse was a vote of confidence in Clayton's future.

Most of the passengers riding the trains did not get off when their train stopped. But some did. They got off to do business in Clayton or bided there a day or two, making arrangements to continue across country on horseback or travel on by coach along the new dirt roads still in the making. Some had picks and shovels and went looking for gold. Others were hoping to find a place to farm and settle, for this was new country, a country for pioneers: you made your claim, farmed it, worked it and fought to keep it. Then there were the cattlemen who stayed only as long as it took to rest their herds before moving on. Clayton was a hard town made by hard men.

But whichever they were, whatever they had come looking for, almost all those who hit town by horse, cart or railroad had a thirst. And the Silver Slipper saloon was the place for killing a thirst. A good time for doing it was on a Saturday, and the best number for it on the dial was around eight o'clock.

The Silver Slipper was full and noisy and doing good business. Tobacco smoke hung in the air and four barkeeps were hardly enough to keep the drinks coming. No one was listening to the piano, especially not the card-players.

A couple or three tables were set aside for them at the back of the room, under the stairs. It was as private as things got on a Saturday in the Silver Slipper. Even so, men loafed around back of the tables, some leaning against the wall, others watching the play

perched on rough-hewn benches pol-
ished smooth by the seats of so many
denim pants.

Daco Ward picked his beer off the bar
top and wandered over to catch some of
the action. He found himself a space on
a bench against a wall, sat down and
while he sipped his beer looked across
at a table where half a dozen men were
examining the hand of cards the dealer
had just sprayed around the green baize
cloth. They made their plays, won, lost,
then played some more.

After a while the piano-dude stopped
playing, got up, stretched, wiped his
forehead with a red kerchief, walked
across to the bar and stuck his face in a
large beer the barkeep had poured for
him.

His place as provider of entertain-
ment was taken by a banjo and fiddle.

No one listened to them either.

Daco fingered the coins in his
pocket. He hadn't reckoned up exactly
but he knew for sure that however
many times he counted his money it

still wouldn't add up to a whole dollar. Seventy cents maybe, and that, together with the clothes he stood up in and the horse he had ridden from Grenidge, 500 miles north of Clayton, was all he had in the world, all he had to show for a dozen years of seeking his fortune.

He had been a cowpoke and a rail-ganger. He'd tried farming and bronco-busting and felling timber. He'd picked up a knowledge of any number of trades along the way and had learned to live off the land and look after himself with his fists. What he had to show for it all amounted to less than a dollar. No one could say worldly success had come knocking at his door.

It didn't bother Daco none. He wasn't a man who sought worldly success. But he wasn't agin' it neither: he liked a soft bed and his dinner on a plate as well as the next man. But along the way he'd learned that life never stays the same way for long. Things just go on changing. They go up and down, they go right and they go wrong. A man moves along sweetly for a spell, with a favourable wind at his back. Then he runs into trouble, falls in a deep pit. Then the kindly wind starts up again, blows him out of the hole he's in and chivvies him along until he gets tripped up again.

So he had less than a dollar. The hell with it. Something would turn up.

He glanced across at the poker players. It looked like a typical game. A hick farmer, cross-eyed with drink, was blowing the cash he'd got for selling his corn. His wife wouldn't like it when he rolled home near broke. A scared-looking rabbit in a tight coat on a dare with himself, afraid to lose, but also scared that he might win, like the feeling and be launched on the road to ruin. An older man in a suit, maybe fifty, could be a patent-medicine sales-man or similar, careful, knew his limits. A guy with fair hair, moustache, younger than Daco but about the same build, in a leather vest and jeans, concentrating hard. The dealer, in shirtsleeves, maybe seventy years of age, wiry, quick hands, a man who had seen it all before.

The last man was big-made, around thirty-five, very black hair slicked down and gleaming with oil, a good line in jokiness between hands. He was doing his practised best to make it look like he was one of the boys but Daco knew he was no such thing. The boots were all wrong. Fine tooled leather, picked out with decorative motifs, expensive. The boots said professional card-player.

The deal was now with the man with slick hair and fancy boots. He dealt a new hand. The rabbit, sweating, looked at his cards, turned white, threw them down, got up and left without a word. The farmer pulled some bills off what was now a thin roll, and tossed them on the table. The rest also bought in.

As the stakes rose the salesman dropped out first, then the farmer's roll gave out, leaving only the guy with the fair hair and the sharper.

Neither man would back down and

the stakes grew higher. There was a lot of money on the table.

Sensing that something big was going down, loafers crowded round as the stakes rose. If Daco had to choose, he'd have put his money on the sharper. Sharpers have professional nerves. Still, the younger man was holding his end up pretty well and Daco found himself wanting the sharper to come off second best.

But not enough to tempt him off his bench and join the crowd now jostling for a ringside view round the table. Anyways, from where he was, he had a clear sight of the table in a mirror hanging off the back wall of the Silver Slipper. It was one of several that the original owners had installed to give the place a touch of class. The mirrors were dirty and the reflections they gave were milky-blue.

But they were clear enough for Daco to get a good sight of the man standing directly behind the player with fair hair: very big, dark hair cropped short, square stubbled jaw, and unblinking grey eyes. There was a lot of pushing and shoving around him as the rednecks craned forward for a better look-see. But the man with the cold grey eyes fended them off and kept his station.

Then, with a piece of sleight of hand that a stage magician would have found hard to beat, he slipped something into the right-hand pocket of the fair-haired player's coat and gave a barely perceptible nod to the sharper sitting opposite.

If Daco hadn't stayed put where he was on the bench he would have missed it. Not just because it had happened so fast but also because the spectators were crowded round close, like peaches in a box, so it was hard to make out anything for certain.

Still Daco didn't move, but he was now alert.

The sharp raised the stakes by another 200. There must now be at least a couple of thousand dollars on the table. There was a good part of the cattleman's wad, the rabbit's last dollar, the medicine man's stake, the old guy's bills plus what the surviving two players had bet.

The man with the blond hair looked the sharp in the eye, laid his 200 on the pile, added another hundred and said:

'I'll see you what you got!'

The sharp paused, put his cards face down on the table, and relit the cheroot that had gone cold in his mouth. He looked at his opponent through the cloud of smoke and smiled.

The men who were crowded round the table fell silent. It was a big call. $2,000 and more were about to find a new home.

Slowly, still not speaking, the sharp turned his cards face up. One by one he revealed four jacks. He smiled and drew on his cheroot, his eyes never leaving the other man's face.

A murmur went up. It was a good hand. A very good hand. But it was a hand that could be beat.

The man with the fair hair put his

cards down with a sudden flourish. Aces that beat those jacks. The watchers gave a shout and the winner's hand was already reaching out to gather up his prize.

'Hold it right there, mister!' the sharp barked.

The fair man's hand stopped. He looked up.

'You're not going to be a poor loser, are you?' he said. 'I took you for a sport.'

'I'm as good a sport as the next man. It's just that I don't like being beat by a man who cheats!'

Ice had suddenly formed in the air of the bar of the Silver Slipper. The knot of men clustered round the table unravelled as the spectators began to back off. No one wanted to be within range when the bullets started flying.

'Say again,' said blondie.

'I say you didn't win that hand fair and square. I say you're a cheat.'

'I sure as hell hope you can back up what you say. Else we're going to have something to settle between us. Private.'

The sharp leaned back on two legs of his chair, flipped his cheroot on to the floor and looked levelly into blondie's eyes.

'I'd lay money you got a special pocket where you keep the cards you don't want. Am I wrong?'

Before anyone had time to react the man who'd been standing behind his chair during the play, the big man with the cropped hair, leaned forward, reached with his hand into blondie's pocket and pulled it out again. Between thumb and forefinger were two cards. He threw them on to the table, face up. King of clubs and ten of diamonds.

'Need any more back-up than that? It's enough for me,' said the sharp.

Surprise showed briefly on blondie's face. Then he smiled.

'Come on, loser man. You know I didn't palm no cards.'

'And how should I know that?'

'Because,' said blondie, 'your sidekick here must have planted them.'

'You can't wriggle out of this,' said the sharp. 'You won that last hand with cards you palmed. Since I was the one you bested, the pot comes to me.'

'First, you can clear up one thing. How come your friend here didn't look up my sleeve or try my other pockets but found a king of clubs and the ten of diamonds in the first place he reached for?'

The sharp held his gaze.

'Beginner's luck. So he stuck in a thumb and pulled out a plum. Don't make a spit of difference: he found the cards, didn't he? Look, you ain't going to talk yourself out of this if that's all the defence you got. You ain't got right on your side, is the top and bottom of it.'

Daco hadn't changed his position. He was still on the bench, now by himself behind blondie. He'd followed the game with interest and hadn't missed the way the sharp had exchanged signals with his confederate, faint nods and winks and fingers raised so carefully you had to be watching very closely or you didn't see them at all.

'Mind if I say a piece?' he said.

Into the heightened silence produced by the confrontation of the two men, Daco's words fell like a pebble dropped into a well from a great height.

'Ain't for me to say, of course, but maybe I can throw some light on what you boys are discussing, help sort out what went wrong here to spoil a good game.'

Blondie turned in his chair and looked at Daco.

'Stay out of this,' barked the sharp, 'it ain't your business . . . '

Daco held up one hand.

'Just being a good citizen,' he said. 'Just wanted to tell what I seen. I know there's not many think the way I do, that it's not a good idea for men to stand too close behind a player's chair when there's a big game going on. It can lead to misunderstandings, maybe to a joke that goes wrong.'

'Joke? What in hell's name you

14

talking about?' snapped the sharp. 'You're the only joke here.'

'What I meant to say,' Daco went on, taking it nice and slow, reducing the pressure, letting the steam out of the situation slowly, 'was this gentleman's joke.'

It was now the turn of the big man with the square jaw to swing round and face Daco.

'You mean me?' he snarled.

'Yes, sir, I sure do, I seen you slip a couple of cards into this man's pocket. You done it so smooth nobody noticed but me. Never saw such a smooth thing. I don't say there was harm intended. But it looks like something went wrong, because it's led to bad trouble.'

'Wait a minute,' said blondie. 'Are you saying you saw this man slip them cards in my pocket?'

'That's what I saw, clear as day.'

'There's your proof, Mister,' blondie said, turning back to the sharp. 'There's a man here could testify in a court of law that I'm telling the truth. I won you fair and square. The pot's mine.'

The sharp's face was white and filled with hate.

Then he relaxed, leaned back in his chair again and laughed.

''Course you won fair and square,' he said and he laughed some more. 'If you could only have seen the look on your face!'

He looked around, as if to share his big joke.

'Go on,' he said to blondie, 'take the pot. It's yours. Beat me fair, aces to jacks. But at least I hope you'll see your way clear to buying your opponent a drink? No hard feelings?' he added, holding out his hand.

'No hard feelings,' said blondie. 'The name's Bill Dodds. Good to know you.'

'Tucker Lankton,' said the sharp. 'And the dude with the tricksy fingers is my associate, Ed Crants.'

'Bartender,' Dodds called across the room, 'bring a bottle over here and some glasses.'

And turning to Daco, who still hadn't moved from the same seat, he said: 'You'll join us too, Mister . . . ?'

'The name's Ward. Daco Ward.'

Daco pulled a chair up to the table and sat opposite Crants. The barkeep brought the bottle.

As it was Dodds's party, he did the pouring.

But it wasn't a very friendly occasion. None of the men around the table was easy, not being of a mind to forget how near to a shooting match they had come.

Lankton knocked back his drink and got to his feet. Crants did likewise.

'Got to go, boys,' he said. 'Business calls. Maybe we'll meet up again? Give me a chance to get my revenge?'

'You can count on it,' said Dodds.

Dodds was left alone with his new friend.

2

An Offer

'I guess a vote of thanks is in order,' said Dodds, as Tucker Lankton and Ed Crants breasted the Silver Slipper's batwing doors and walked out into the now dark street.

'Ain't necessary,' said Daco, taking a pull on his glass. 'Just did what anyone who'd seen a piece of dirty play would have done.'

'Maybe, but it was two against one and I never knew a thing about the partner Lankton had a couple of inches from my back. I'd have been in a tight spot if you hadn't spoken up. When he said revenge, he sure wasn't talking about getting a chance to win his money back at cards. More I think, the less I like the odds that I would have gotten out of that fix without picking up at least a couple of holes in my hide.'

Daco made a dismissive gesture and stood up.

'You bought me a drink. That takes care of all the thanks I need.'

'Don't go, Daco. I got a proposition for you.'

'Fire away,' said Daco, sitting down as Dodds refilled his glass.

'I'm in Clayton on business. I got no choice but to hang around town until the shipment I'm expecting comes through. I don't know exactly which train it'll come in on, but it's due any day. Now, I got a feeling I ain't seen the last of Tucker Lankton and his sidekick. Tucker don't look like the sort who forgets that he's got bested and I'd say Crants was a man with a mean streak running right through him. They know I got a couple of thousand dollars in my inside pocket and I reckon I'm top of the list of the business they said they had to take care of. Am I making sense to you?'

'Plenty sense. If I was in your shoes

I'd be keeping my hand on my gun and watching my back.'

'I'd say you've got cause to watch yours too, Daco. After all, if you hadn't blown a hole in their story, they'd have had me cold.'

'So what are you saying to me, Bill?'

'A proposition. Like I said, I got business in Clayton. I'm picking up supplies to haul up country, out Pocaloca way. Three-day trip. It's a lonely trail and three days is a long time for a man to be watching his back. What say you come along for the ride? You'll get your coffee and bacon and beans on the road and a job when you get there, if you want one. We sure could use an extra pair of hands at Pocaloca.'

'What sort of work would that be?'

'Gold claim. Not a mine, so no tunnel work. Pick and shovel mostly, and some panning. The operation's paying well so far.'

'How many working the claim?'

'Three,' said Dodds, 'and good men. You'd fit in, no question of it.'

Whether he would or not didn't come into it. When a man's got seventy cents between him and broke, he don't waste time on the finer points.

'Good man,' said Dodds. 'Got a place to stay?'

'Hadn't exactly got round to fixing one up.'

'Good, you can use the same place as me. It'll be safer for us both if we stick together. Come on, we can get something to eat there.'

Casey's Rooming House was a two storey clapboard building. It was painted white and was as clean inside as it looked from the outside. Dodds had a room on the first floor with a veranda and a view of the street. Daco was two doors along the corridor but on the opposite side overlooking the stables and the yard out back. When they'd eaten, they told each other good night and went to their separate quarters.

Daco sat on the bed — he hadn't slept in a bed in a long while — and thought about his luck which had held

21

again. He'd drifted into Clayton with just enough money in his pocket to buy a drink and here he was, inside four good walls, with a good meal under his belt and a job. But he didn't think about it for too long because he was dog- tired. The room was warm, his belly was full, the bed was comfortable and, shutting his ears to the ruckus coming from the Silver Slipper and leaving tomorrow to take care of itself, he was soon asleep.

And dreaming.

He dreamed he was back in Brooklands, Colorado, where he'd grown up. He was in his grandma's house. His grandma had raised him after his ma and pa had been killed in an Indian raid. She had a sharp tongue, used a strap on him and was a lousy cook. But she was all the family he had and her house the nearest thing to home he'd known. He was never given the chance to be a boy and do boys' things with other boys. She drove him hard, expecting him to put in a full day's work on the homestead which was their livelihood. He had grown up when he was still young, old beyond his years with having to look out for himself. And now he was back in that house.

It was empty. There were cobwebs. Grandma could not abide bugs and hated cobwebs. So she wasn't around the place. Nobody was there. The brown photo of his ma and pa on their wedding day still hung over the chimney piece. The chairs and table were exactly where they used to be. But nothing was quite right. The room wasn't quite square for a start and the window was on the wrong wall and something was scratching at the door. Maybe a raccoon was sharpening its claws on the doorjamb. But Daco suddenly knew it wasn't because he was wide awake.

He wasn't in his grandma's deserted old house back in Brooklands, Colorado, but here in Clayton Creek, Box Tree County, and the noise wasn't coming from the door of his grandma's homestead but from the door of his room in Casey's Rooming House.

The street outside had gone quiet, so Daco reckoned the night was well advanced, probably near morning, because on Saturday nights the party wasn't over until the last man standing fell over.

The moon was up and its glow cast just enough light for Daco to have his bearings.

The noise stopped, then started again. Someone was picking the lock. Quietly, Daco slipped out of bed and pulled on his pants and gunbelt. Hurriedly he made a hump of the blankets to make the bed look as if a man was sleeping in it then took up a position behind the thin curtains that covered the windows and gave enough shadow to hide him. He settled down to see what would happen next. He wasn't kept waiting long.

The scratching started up again. After a while there was a click as the

deadbolt was pulled back and everything went quiet again. Slowly, the door
opened. The intruder took a moment to
get his bearings and then made silently
for the bed. Something gleamed at the
end of his right arm and it caught the
moonlight as he raised it then brought
it down savagely on the huddled shape
under the blanket. Twice more he
struck in rapid succession and then
stopped, surprised by the lack of
resistance met by the blade of his
hunting knife. He yanked back the
sheets and froze when he saw what he
had attacked: a couple of pillows.

'Put the knife down,' said Daco as he
stepped out from behind the curtain,
gun in hand. 'I got the drop on you.'

The knife made a thunk as it hit the
floor.

'Step into the light,' said Daco, 'so I
can get a proper look at you.'

A pair of hand-tooled cowboy boots
walked into the bars of moonlight that
entered by the window. They kept
coming. The bars crept up a body. First

they revealed a gun slung in a classy holster on the man's left hip and then the face and slicked-down hair of Tucker Lankton.

'That's far enough. Now, take the gun out, slowly, and toss it on the bed.'

The belt and holster were fancy, but the well-worn wooden butt made the gun a real working weapon.

'What's your game, Lankton? You want the money so bad you'd kill for it? Or is it you're just sore at losing your play?'

Before Tucker Lankton could open his mouth to frame a reply, there was a crash of broken glass behind Daco and an arm reached in through the broken window pane, knocking his gun from his hand. As he turned, he saw Ed Crants burst in and aim a swing at him. If it had landed it would have sent Daco to sleep for a month. But he pulled his head back in time and Crants's fist whistled past his chin, meeting nothing solid, only air. The impetus threw him off balance and

Daco caught him with a chopping right to the side of the head which sent him crashing over the bed on to the floor in a daze.

Daco sized up the situation: it was the two-flank trick. Lankton had gone in through Casey's front door and walked up the stairs, while Crants had gone round the back and climbed on to the roof of the stables which put him outside Daco's window. He was wondering how they'd known which room he'd be in when Lankton lunged towards him, trying to grab him.

Daco stuck out his left, fending him off while he thought fast. Somebody must have heard the crash of breaking glass, but no one was coming to ask why. That didn't surprise him overmuch, because Clayton was still enough of a frontier town for folks to keep their heads under the blankets when they heard sounds of battle at night. But where was Dodds? Why wasn't he riding to the rescue? Had they got to him first?

His next thought was that there were too many guns in the room. There was Lankton's revolver and Daco's Colt, now somewhere on the floor, not to mention whatever Crants was carrying, to say nothing of the knife Lankton had used. If he didn't get his hands on a weapon soon he could kiss his chances goodbye, for he was facing two men who clearly did not wish him well.

Daco stopped jabbing and drove a right into Lankton's face, hard. He felt it grind his lips against his teeth. Then he crossed with another right that spun him against the wall. As his man retreated, Daco advanced, feeling with his bare feet for one of the guns that had been spilled on to the floor and keeping one eye on Crants, who was getting to his feet, shaking his head to clear it, and looking furious.

Daco's two assailants were between him and the door. He backed to the window and cursed himself for not having spied out the lie of the land more carefully and worked out an escape route. He'd been a fool not to expect that Lankton would probably make a play of some sort, and now he was paying for being careless. He glanced through the window over his shoulder and confirmed what he vaguely remembered. The roof of the stables reached up to within a few feet of his windowsill, then sloped down to where a couple of carts stood in the yard. It would be best if he could make it to the door and then get out down the stairs: he'd be a sitting target if he tried going out through the window, down the roof and on to a cart. In the time that would take, he could get shot many times over.

In the back.

And then Crants came on to him. He wasn't great shakes as a fighter but he was big and strong. He swung wildly with a right that would have felled a horse. Daco got inside him, planting a left straight on his nose and following it up with a right to the body. When Crants dropped his guard, Daco caught him with a right hook to his cheek that cut to the bone. As Crants staggered back Lankton moved in. He caught Daco off balance and scored a snapping left to the ear and then crossed with a right to the heart that took his breath away.

But Daco went on jabbing with his left and kept Lankton at a distance until his legs felt right again. Then he moved forward, dodging and feinting and getting under Lankton's guard with a series of solid blows to the stomach. As his man turned away, Daco caught him with a big right hand to the kidney. As soon as he landed it, he knew he'd hit the spot and that Lankton was out of it. No one gets up when he takes a sweet, full-weight punch to the kidneys.

He turned to face Crants, who was on his feet again. Crants was gulping for air, not on account of his exertions but because of his split nose and pulpy lips, which made it hard for him to breathe. He ducked his head and charged, arms flailing. Daco chopped at him, cutting and stabbing him with accurate punches, but he couldn't stop the big man who by chance managed to grab his left hand and hang on to it, twisting it in the hope of pinioning his opponent. He bent down and suddenly Daco found himself flying through the air. He crashed into the wall and collapsed, winded, in a heap on the floor. Before he could reassemble his wits Crants was on him, wading in with boots and fists. Unable to get up or defend himself, Daco curled up into a ball and waited until he passed out or the big man ran out of steam, whichever happened first.

He didn't have to wait that long.

He raised his arms to protect his head. As he did so, his right hand brushed against something hard and cool and smooth that lay flush against the base of the wall. It was a gun. Maybe it wasn't his. Maybe it was Lankton's. Either way it was a gun and he reached for it.

It fitted snugly into his fist. The

trigger could have been made to fit his finger.

Crants hadn't run out of steam yet. His boots went on smashing into the body of the smaller man who had ceased to put up any resistance. A kick in the small of the back made Daco tense up against the pain. His muscles went into spasm and without his meaning it his trigger finger tightened and the gun went off.

The detonation lit up the room, its brilliance blinding the three men. The sound tore into the silence of the night, driving it to the four corners of the world. And then the room was black again, and blacker than before after the brilliance of the flash. The silence surged back, though now it was spiked with sounds. Dogs barked, cocks crowed, doors banged and a voice shouted for whoever it was to shut the hell up, there were people here trying to get some sleep.

Daco sat up and waved the gun around, looking for anything that moved.

'Back off, Crants,' he snapped, guided by the sound of the big man's heavy breathing. 'Move over to the window so I can get a better sight of you. And take Lankton with you.'

He heard the big man retreat. Already his night vision was returning and he made out Crants stoop down and haul his partner to his feet.

Daco sat up, leaning his aching back against the wall. He pointed the gun in the general direction of the sound made by Crants as he dragged the groaning Lankton to the window. In those swollen and trembling hands his grip on the gun was none too sure. He wouldn't have laid out folding money on being able to shoot straight. Then he did something that was really hard.

He stood up.

True, he cheated some. He used the frame of the bed to pull himself upright and then clung on to the wall for dear life to stay vertical. But what the hell, he made it.

He saw two silhouettes move into the

window frame against the near-morning sky, which had begun to lighten.

'OK,' he said, putting as much steel in his voice as he could manage. 'Now you can tell me what this is all about or I blow your heads off.'

'Look, mister,' said Crants, 'I don't know nothing. I guess you just got in the way of something that was going down. My partner here, he's the one who could tell you, but he's in no shape for having a conversation. What did you hit him with? He's still out of it . . . '

And then Crants leaned back and fell out of the shattered window through which he had come in, taking Lankton with him. Daco heard them roll down the stable roof and land with a thump in one of the standing carts.

He moved his stiff carcass across the room as fast as he could, though it felt as though he was walking through glue, and looked out of the window. He was just in time to see Crants, with Lankton on his shoulder, disappear out of the yard and make off down the street. He loosed off a shot without much hope of hitting either of them, just to let them know not to come back.

He put the gun down on the bed and sat down next to it. He felt his back, his arms, his legs. He was sore everywhere but nothing seemed to be broken. But his feet felt wet. In the early morning light, he could see they were covered with blood which was now congealing. That's what you get from walking on broken windowpanes with no boots on.

He was still picking shards of glass out of his lacerated soles when Casey walked in through the open door.

3

Casey's Boarding-House

He came in swearing damnations and brandishing a big gun, a large man, with a red face and a gammy leg.

'What in Hades's been going on here?' he asked as he surveyed the wreckage.

Daco sat in the middle of it. The blankets on the bed were in shreds and straw from the mattress littered the floor. The end of the bed had collapsed, a clothes-press that Crants had smashed into had been reduced to matchwood and there was a hole in the ceiling where Daco's bullet had passed through it and brought the plaster down. The window was just a hole in the wall. The wind blew through it and made the thin curtains dance a jig. And there was blood on the walls and on the floor, most of it Daco's.

Daco gestured weakly to the window. Casey walked across and looked out.

'So they beat it, huh? You all right?' he asked, putting his gun down.

Daco nodded. He went on pulling glass out of his right foot.

'How d'ya feel?'

'Sore. Like I'd been put in a barrel with a lot of rocks and rolled down a hill.'

'Looks like it was some fight,' said Casey, fishing for details.

'Sure was. Two of 'em. Guy called Tucker Lankton and his sidekick name of Crants. Crants came in the window. Lankton walked up the stairs. You should keep your front door locked at night, Casey. You could lose a lot of customers leaving it open for anyone to come in off the street and murder them in their beds. You notice any other variety of ruckus going on in this establishment?'

'Nope. All quiet until that first shot went off.'

'Look, Casey, let's save the details for later. Just for now you'd oblige me by stepping outside and knocking on my partner's door, across the hall. If Lankton and Crants came looking for anyone, it was him they wanted, not me. If you heard the shot, why didn't he? Why ain't he in here?'

Casey didn't move.

'Because he's gone,' he said.

'Gone? Gone where?'

'Didn't say. I was just shutting up last thing, after everybody had gone to bed, around midnight it would have been, when he comes down, bag packed and all ready to go. Said to tell you he'd changed his mind about the trip. Said to tell you sorry. But to make up for it, he left fifty dollars to take care of your expenses. I got it safe downstairs for you. Seems like,' he said, looking around the room costing the devastation with his hotelier's eye, 'the fifty will cover the damage.'

Daco did not reply. His mind was working fast.

What had happened to make Dodds change his mind about wanting him to ride bodyguard on the drive back to Pocaloca? Say Dodds had a good reason for not wanting him hanging around. So he decides to get out. Then say Lankton really wanted to get even for being outsmarted in the Silver Slipper: wouldn't he have followed them to Casey's and found out that was where they were holed up for the night? And say Dodds had walked out of Casey's front door and run straight into Lankton who was waiting, got himself beat up and spilled which room Daco was staying at. That was an explanation that fitted the facts.

Or was the plan a set-up from the start? Had Dodds sold him out to Lankton because they were somehow in cahoots? That would figure too; it fitted the facts just as well, if you allowed that thieves can fall out over a card game and allowing that Lankton and Dodds were thieves both. This was getting deep. He needed more facts before he was going to get any further with it.

'You see which way Dodds headed off?' he asked. He tore strips off the shredded bed cover and used them as a bandage for his cut feet.

'Nope. He just took his carpetbag and turned left out the door.'

'Towards the railroad depot?'

'Could be.'

'Was there a train due in last night?'

'Sure was. One came through, going west, about two in the morning.'

Daco reached for his shirt, buckled his pants on and pulled his boots over his bandaged feet. He stood up and tested them. He felt sore all over. So did his feet. But he could live with it.

'Would there be enough left of those fifty dollars to pay for breakfast?' he asked.

'Sure, and then some left over,' said Casey, with a good-humoured laugh. 'Just give me ten minutes and I'll rustle you up a breakfast like you never saw. Bacon, eggs and a hunk of Mrs Casey's best new-baked warm bread do you?'

And with a pot of Casey's hot coffee to wash it down, it was a breakfast to put back what had been taken out and set a man up for the day.

By the time Daco stepped out into Clayton's main street, with twenty of Dodds's dollars that remained after deductions for a night's board plus breakages, he could feel the strength surging back into him. True, he ached and his cut feet were sore, but that would pass. Walking soon got his muscles working and the blood flowing, so that by the time he got to the rail depot the effects of the night's brawl had more or less worn off. He drew a few looks from the town's early risers, for his right cheek was swollen and his lower lip was split. He didn't look pretty but he felt good.

At the depot he asked for the official who'd been on night duty, a middle-aged man with a paunch, a gaucho moustache and a Union Pacific Railroad cap.

'Fair hair, thirty or thereabouts, good

height, meaning about the size of you? Waiting to collect a delivery on the night train going west? And who might be wanting to know?' he said, lifting his cap and scratching his head. 'Railroad business is private. 'Sides, it's real dark around two in the morning, so dark you cain't hardly tell if a man's fair-haired and thirty and a goodly size or bald, eighty and a midget.'

'Partner of mine. He was in town to collect supplies we was supposed to be carting up country today, but there's no sign of him this morning,' said Daco, pulling a couple of bills from his waistcoat pocket.

'Now you put it like that,' said the official, 'I can feel something definitely coming back to me, but it's still a mite cloudy around the edges.'

'So I got to worrying and came directly here on the off chance someone might have seen him,' Daco went on smoothly, producing another two dollars.

'Fair hair, well set-up, wearing a

leather vest, jeans, boots and no spurs. Picture is as clear as day,' said the official, taking the bills and folding them into his back pocket. 'I seen him plenty times. A week he's been coming here for his goods and last night they came. A wooden case. Very heavy. Asked me to lock it up secure for an hour while he went for his rig. He came back with the rig, loaded up and that's the last I saw of him.'

'Know what was in the case?'

'I can guess, but I ain't saying. Against the rules.'

'Where'd he go to get his rig?'

'You sure want a lot of questions answering for your money, son,' the official sighed. 'Try Elmer Gamble's, two streets on the far side of the Silver Slipper. Now that's all I can remember. Memory's gone again. It gets like that the older you get. It jest comes and goes. There's no helping it.'

'You must keep a record of what freight arrives, who sent it and who collects it? Could I see that?'

'Nope. That's highly confidential company information.'

Daco produced a five-dollar bill and waved it under the man's nose.

'Maybe the smell of this will make you forget to lock your office door so I could slip in and have me a look-see in your record book?'

The man hesitated, then reached for the money.

'On my desk. You got five minutes while I go and answer a sudden call of nature. Good doing business with you, son.'

The ledger was open. Forty-six passengers had boarded the 2 a.m. train, thirty-seven had got off and seventeen items of freight had been unloaded. A wooden barrel, weight 150 pounds, had been signed for by W. Dodds, addressed to Clayton depot, for collection. It had been shipped from St Louis by the Wexley Gunpowder Co.

Daco stared at the entry. Supplies? Dodds had said the claim wasn't a mine but a pick and shovel, washing-and-panning operation. You didn't need a large keg of gunpowder for that kind of set-up.

So Dodds hadn't levelled with him. He left the ledger as he'd found it and walked out of the official's office with questions crowding into his mind.

He knew exactly where Elmer Gamble's livery stable was located. Before having supper with Dodds he'd parked his black stallion there for the night. Elmer was more forthcoming than the railroad man had been. In reply to Daco's questions, he said sure he remembered Bill Dodds, fair guy, with a moustache. Who wouldn't remember a guy who came and woke the place up in the middle of the night wanting his rig made ready and his bill made up. Seemed in a mighty hurry. Buckboard wagon drawn by a single horse. Decent piece of horseflesh. Too good to be pulling a rig. Headed off towards the railroad depot, saying he was going to pick up a piece of freight he'd been waiting for that had come on the night train. But nope, he didn't know where he'd gone after that. That's OK, think nothing of it, happy to oblige, and do you want your horse?

Daco rode slowly back to Casey's with his head still full of unanswered questions, foremost of which was: why am I working up a worry over this business anyway? This time yesterday I had less than a dollar. Today, even after paying Elmer and the railroad man, I got more than ten and a full belly. That puts me ahead.

What's it to me if a man I never met before promises me a job and gives me fifty dollars. It ain't the first time a man's made me an offer of a job that never came to nothing. And fifty dollars ain't over the odds as a gratuity for helping a man keep hold of the $2,000 he's won fair and square in a poker game. No, there's nothing to be fretting over in any of this. There's also a simple explanation for the early morning visit he'd received: Lankton was just plain sore about what happened in the Silver Slipper and wanted his revenge.

But if he was just sore, he could have had Daco beaten up by his man Crants. Only a madman or someone with a bigger motive than payback would try to kill the bystander who'd put a spoke in his wheel, it wouldn't be worth anybody's while tangling with the law to do that. Now Lankton didn't strike Daco as being mad, so maybe there was more to this business than met the eye. And then there was the timing. Lankton had come looking for Daco long after Dodds had left town. Maybe he'd gone to Casey's to get his retribution, found Dodds gone and then decided to take it out on Daco in his frustration. Maybe he figured Daco was closer to Dodds than he really was, like a partner in some venture.

The more he thought, the crazier it all seemed. What in tarnation was Dodds doing driving a rig with a keg of gunpowder on board across the desert to a gold claim that was a level job, not a mine?

But most of all, Daco didn't like the feeling that Dodds had taken him for a ride, had lied to him.

When he got back to Casey's, Casey looked up from washing glasses behind his bar and said:

'Got someone you ought to talk to. Clip! Come on out here!'

From out back an old timer came in the room, maybe seventy years of age, stooping and wizened, with pale blue, rheumy eyes and a shuffling walk.

'This here's Clip Dougan. He's my night man. I pay the old fool to sit behind the counter and keep a general eye on things. I don't know what he does exactly. Sleeps most of the time, I bet. I do know he brings a bottle to work with him regular. The idea is that he's the guy on hand if any of the guests need anything after I've closed up and gone to bed. Mrs Casey also made me give him a gun. She figures if a man has some kind of gun, that makes him a guard. Makes her feel safer. To me, old Clip is more likely to shoot hisself in the foot than late night marauders. Still, you should talk to him.'

'I was shooting marauders when you was still wetting your pants, Casey,' said Clip. Then turning to Daco: 'The name's Bob, Bob Dougan, not Clip. Know why they call me Clip? 'Cos one day, Jim Bridger — you've heard tell of Jim Bridger, the Mountain Man? course you have — well one day, Jim Bridger says, talking about me . . .'

' . . . look at the way that boy goes at things, at a helluva clip!' said Casey, finishing the old man's sentence, which he'd heard so often, for him.

'Sure he did. That's exactly what he said. And the name just stuck. Now what can I do for you, young fella?'

'You can tell me about last night. You were here on duty, right? Man walks in, maybe four o'clock, aged around thirty, slicked back hair, fancy gunbelt. He pull a gun?'

'Nope. He just asked which room Dodds had. I said seven and up he went.'

'Dodds was in six. I was in seven.'

'Yup. Won't argue with you. My mistake.'

Daco paused. So there'd been no contact between Dodds and Lankton. He'd been targeted because an old timer had got a room number wrong.

'You tell him Dodds wasn't here?' he said.

'Nope. He never asked.'

'So he never went near the room Dodds was in?'

'Nope.'

'Did you see or hear anything else?'

'Sure I heard things. It was a quiet night. But I didn't just hear owls and coyotes. About an hour after friend Dodds lit out of here with his bag, I heard a wagon come up the street. I look out the front window there and what do I see?'

He paused for effect.

'Dodds driving a rig, heading out of

town. He pulls up just outside, comes in and walks up the stairs, just as if he was going back to his room. But he wasn't gone more than a minute. Then he comes down again carrying a leather bag, a kind of satchel. Looked heavy but not too heavy. Then he went out again. Never said a word but threw the bag on the back of the rig and drove off. But that wasn't all I saw.'

He paused again. Casey snorted with impatience.

'Next, maybe an hour after Dodds left, the dude with the slicked-down hair went up and I heard the ruckus in number seven, then the shot, then bodies rolling down the stable roof, then another shot. I have me a look out of the side window there and what do I see?'

'Just tell the man what you saw, Clip. This ain't the time for play-acting.'

'Two *hombres*, the big one half-carrying the dude who didn't look like he could walk without help. Down the street they went until they got to the

Silver Slipper. I seen 'em go in. I never seen 'em come out again until they rode past maybe a half hour since.'

'Which way did they go?' asked Daco quickly.

'South. Same way as friend Dodds. Had bedrolls tied behind their saddles and saddle-bags that looked like they was carrying supplies. Looked like they wasn't counting on coming back for a spell.'

Somehow Lankton had found out, most likely from Elmer Gamble, that Dodds had collected his rig and driven out of Clayton. So they'd gone after him. Daco now knew that he'd been right: there was more to this feud than a poker game.

'Ever heard of a place called Pocaloca?' he asked.

Casey thought for a moment: 'Name don't mean a thing to me,' he said. 'How about you, Clip?'

The old man furrowed his brow.

'I ain't used to all this talking. Mouth's gone so dry I can hardly speak.'

'Give him a drink, Casey. On me,' said Daco with a smile. 'He's being very helpful and I wouldn't want him to go straining his voice or any other part of himself on my account.'

Casey poured a shot and held it out to the old timer who downed it in one. He smacked his lips, set the empty glass down and came up with his side of the bargain.

'Sure I heard of Pocaloca. Small place, about a three-day ride from here. Take the road south and follow it for a day and a half till you see a sign that says ten miles to Chisholm. Just after that there's a trail that takes you off west towards a line of hills. Them's the foothills of the Galejadas mountains and Pocaloca is the biggest town in the county. Not that there's much to it, a store, a livery stable, coupla holding pens for sheep — there's no grazing for cattle — and maybe half a dozen houses along a street. I had a girl there once . . . '

'Anyone ever go looking for gold in

Pocaloca?' asked Daco.

'Where there's mountains, there's always somebody looking for gold,' said Casey.

'Never came across anything like that when I was there,' said Clip. 'But that was over thirty years ago, so I'd be talking out of turn if I say no one was looking. Mind you, I did hear tell of an old timer who struck silver in the heights back of the town, must be forty years since. The claim paid off to start with but then dried up. But I never heard about anybody doing big on gold in that neck of the woods. Silveroo. That's what they called the place where the old timer had his claim. On maps they call it Shu'quuit pass. Everybody roundabout knows it as Silveroo.'

Daco's doubts vanished. His curiosity was roused. What was Dodds up to? Why was Lankton so interested? He made up his mind.

'Casey, I'm going to pay a visit to Pocaloca. I got a bedroll. Could you get me some provisions together? Enough for three days.'

'Sure,' said Casey. 'Pay me when you get back. Till then, I'll stake you.'

'Best give him your biggest size of canteen, Casey. It's dry country and hot, not the sort of place you want to be without water.'

With his head full of unanswered questions, Daco went up to his still rough-housed room and got his few possessions together.

4

Ambushed

Reckoning by Clip Dougan's account of the night's events, it must have been around three in the morning when Dodds left town. He'd be well away by now and, Daco thought, heading for Pocaloca. Where else would he go? Lankton and Crants had followed four or five hours later, while Daco had been making enquiries at the rail depot, which made it maybe an hour since. That gave Dodds a big start on them.

Dodds in his rig would be slow but Lankton and Crants had fresh horses and would be travelling fast — though maybe not all that fast if Lankton was still feeling the effects of the sweet punch Daco had landed on him. It must have at least bruised his kidneys and might have cracked a rib. Riding a horse sure ain't a cure for a busted side.

The sun was well up and already hot. But it would get a lot hotter as the day wore on. At this season, the rivers and streams were dry and no cattle could be moved south over the flat, unending plain until the land greened up again in the autumn rain. The going would get tougher not easier the further he went, though water would be his biggest problem. He had extra canteens for himself and his horse, and more ammo than he usually carried for his .44 and the Winchester. So he didn't push it but took Blackie along at a jogging trot which soon turned into a lope. A wolf couldn't have maintained so regular a pace, making maybe six miles an hour.

He'd won the stallion in a poker game in Denver. Blackie stood fifteen hands high and weighed maybe 1,000 pounds. There were bigger horses, stronger too, but not many that were smarter or had such big hearts. Blackie wasn't a ride: he was a friend.

For the first mile or so he passed

occasional riders and wagons heading into town. But after that he saw no one. The trail was clear. He could make out the wheel-marks of a rig which he figured was Dodds's. He could also see the tracks of two horses.

After a couple of hours, the sun had climbed high in the sky and the land had begun to shimmer in the heat. He rode on until he spied a low rocky outcrop to his left and made straight for it. In its shade he caught up on some sleep and rested Blackie until the sun began to wester. Then he moved on again, though not until the cool of the evening had settled on the earth and the moon was up to show him the way.

Having decided to travel by night and avoid the heat of the day he made steady progress. By morning, the character of the land had changed again. It was rockier now and the road rose and fell as it crossed broad folds in the earth. There was more cover hereabouts and Daco found good shade to rest up during the hot time. But he felt exposed. He kept his eyes open. If Lankton and Crants spied him coming after them they could hide up in these rocks and pick him off. He had no intention of letting himself be shot at. The way it turned out, he wasn't the one who got caught off his guard.

The sun was going down and the heat had lost its fierce edge when he saddled up Blackie and resumed his journey. After an hour or so, he turned off the main trail at the sign Clip had told him about, the one saying ten miles to Chisholm. The high Galejadas rose dead ahead and already he could make out the lower slopes covered with pine, live oaks and dark-green bushes.

Suddenly he caught the scent of wood smoke and reined in. Dismounting, he hitched Blackie in a stand of mesquite and went forward on foot. As he advanced, the pungency of the smoke was challenged by the smell of coffee. Then Daco heard a horse snort. He rounded a boulder, gun in fist, and then stopped. The buckboard was there and Dodds was bending over a fire. He looked up, started and then relaxed.

'Daco! What in tarnation you doing here?'

'I've come to get some answers, Bill. To start with, I'd like to know what made you change your mind so you ran out on me.'

'Put the gun up, take the weight off your feet and have some chow — '

'Stow it, Bill, this ain't no picnic. You see anything of Lankton?'

'No, why should I?'

'Cos he's coming after you like he came after me. I don't know what he wants but he sure is fired up.'

Daco, reassured by Dodds's easy reactions, holstered the Colt and told how Lankton and Crants had jumped him in Casey's and how they'd ridden out of Clayton only hours after Dodds had taken his rig and headed south.

'I didn't pass Lankton and Crants on the road,' said Daco, 'so I don't see how I could have got ahead of them. I don't like the feeling that they're out there, in the dark, writing our names on bullets. Or maybe they went straight on to Chisholm. Could be they decided to water their horses there. Maybe Lankton was feeling bad and needed to rest up.'

'Or maybe they rode on to Chisholm and took the road from there that heads due west to Pocaloca. It joins this trail about five miles further on. That way they'd get ahead of me. Could be they're up there waiting to jump us.'

'So we'll take no chances,' said Daco, kicking sand over the fire until it was out. 'But there's no point in wasting good coffee, seeing as how it's made.'

While he drank his coffee and ate a plate of jerked beef and biscuit, Dodds told him the rest. He came clean. He had no partners at Pocaloca. After the card game, which had been a bad mistake, he'd reckoned Lankton would make trouble, and too much was riding on his visit to town for him to let that happen. He'd wanted a good man to watch out for him, so he'd spun a yarn to bring Daco on board.

'What exactly was riding on it? But first, tell me what made you change your mind and leave town?'

'After you bunked down for the night, I got to thinking that since Lankton hadn't made a move, he had most likely cooled off and put my name lower down his list of important things to do. A fella like him has always got things to do, not always legit things, and I figured he wouldn't want any trouble that would interfere with business. What clinched it was that my supplies arrived on the night train. I'd been checking every train that got in and now I had my goods I had no reason to hang around town any more. Before I went I left some money for you with Casey. It was my way of saying thanks for helping me out and sorry about the job. I hope it was enough?'

'No complaints there,' said Daco, 'but that don't explain why your supplies had gunpowder written on the package.'

Dodds took the makings out of his vest pocket and rolled himself a smoke, lit it, inhaled deeply and settled back against the wheel of the rig to tell his tale.

'My folks came to Pocaloca from St Louis. Ma was a piano-teacher and Pa was a professional man, trained to be a land surveyor. I never got the full story but there was some argufying between their families, who were against them marrying. So they left home, headed west and fetched up in Pocaloca. Built themselves a house on a spot Pa chose and over the years they turned into sheep-farmers They get a lot of rain up there, on account of it being mountain country. We came along, I mean me and my sister Annie, and we was a family. Then two years back Pa was killed in an accident. His horse fell on him. With him gone, things got harder. We survived but it wasn't an easy life. We had to lay off the hired help and all the work fell on us.

'Anyways, I was riding out one day,

chasing lost sheep, when my horse put a foot on a gopher hole and threw me. I must have hit my head because I passed out. When I came to I was lying on my back in a heap of scree at the bottom of a high rock face. The sun was hot. I turned my head to stop it shining in my eyes. My horse was there, grazing a few yards off. But between me and it the ground seemed to be lit up here and there. I raised myself on one elbow, shook my head to clear it, blinked and reached out my hand for one of those shining stones. And this is what it was.'

Dodds reached into his pocket and from it took what could have been a small hazelnut. It gleamed dully as he held it up to the moonlight.

'Gold!' he said softly.

Daco took the nugget, rolled it round in his fingers and whistled.

'Just scattered among the rocks and shining like stars,' said Dodds. 'Judging by the way they lay, being well spaced out, they had fallen from a height. I tried to see where from exactly, but there were bushes growing out all the way up the bluff and I couldn't make anything out. The face was too smooth to climb, but I knew I had to get to the top and check out my find.

'I got on my horse and followed the line of the bluff looking for a way up. I rode for mebbe an hour. I saw plenty more scree but nothing else gleamed in it. Then just as I was thinking I'd have to go home and get ropes and go up the hard way, there was a sudden break in the rock wall: a cave. The gap was overgrown but I could make out what looked like the bars of a gate. It was all snarled up with bushes but I got it open and took a look inside.

'It was big enough inside to hold a whole flock of sheep. That's what Pa had used it for, as a holding pen for when the weather was bad or there were wolves prowling around. It was empty now, of course, and I couldn't see how far back it went. But I did recognize some of Pa's stuff lying around, stores the mice had got at but also some of his tools: a pickaxe, shovel and crowbar, all with his initials on. Now a sheepman don't in the ordinary way of things have much use for crowbars in his work. So I looked some more and at the back of the cave I found some diggings. So I put two and two together. He'd found this cave, used it as a refuge for the sheep. Then one day he'd noticed a rock formation that meant something to him. Could only have been gold. Pa was a surveyor, so he knew about rocks. He must have just started working on it when he was killed. Never said anything to us, I expect for fear of raising our hopes too high.'

'But it don't sound like he found the scree with the nuggets you chanced across,' said Daco. 'He knew about rocks, so he'd have told straight off if it was fool's gold or real. If it was the genuine article, he wouldn't have held back. He'd have cashed in and you'd have had hired hands around the place again.'

'You're right. But I never told Ma and Annie about what I'd found neither, no more than he did. Wanted to be sure first. So after thinking a while what was best to do, I made a bag of Pa's diggings along with a handful of them choice nuggets and rode into Clayton Creek. They got an assay office there.'

'And?'

'Turns out it's the real stuff all right. And it's good grade ore, too.'

'So you sold some gold?'

'Sure. I was strapped. I had expenses.'

'Then started throwing your money around?' asked Daco sharply.

'No, sir!' said Dodds. 'I figured I'd need gunpowder if I was going into the mining business. But I didn't want to attract attention and word goes round quick if there's the slightest sniff of a gold strike. So instead of buying it in Clayton I telegraphed to St Louis for it. But I did buy a rig. No avoiding it. But that wasn't suspicious. There's people buying rigs every day of the week. Then

I just sat tight and waited for my goods to come.'

Daco sighed.

'Bill, you couldn't have acted more dumb. Clayton's one of those places where dudes hang out waiting for greenhorns like you to come along. A guy like Lankton always has one spy in the assay office, another in the bank and anything he wants to know about railroad business he gets by greasing a railroad man's palm. Just like I did. He had you marked down as easy meat from the moment you showed up in the assay office waving your bag of samples like you were practising semaphore.'

'I was very careful!'

'Careful? The first thing you told me, a perfect stranger, was that you and your partners had struck it rich. I can see it now. Lankton came on to you, didn't he? Nice and friendly, wasn't he? Talked you into a card game, picks a quarrel, takes you outside and tells you to choose between a bullet or coughing up the location of your strike. Get this straight, Bill, Lankton knows about your strike and he ain't going to let go until he's got his hands on it.'

Dodds fell silent. What Daco said fitted the facts of the case. Then he said:

'You still want that job?'

'Count me in,' said Daco with a grin. 'I ain't come this far without wanting to know how it all finishes up. Besides, if we play it right, at the end of the road there's gold just lying there waiting for a man's hand to pick it up. Come on, let's go.'

They struck camp. Daco hitched Blackie to the back of the buckboard, got up beside Dodds and took the reins. The trail was deserted and there were no recent tracks in it: they had the night to themselves.

The moon was up now and a cool wind made travelling now as easy as it would be hard under the noonday sun. The road picked its way through broken terrain. There was plenty of cover and Daco stayed alert. But when it came, the surprise was complete.

Without warning, a man stepped out into the road from behind a rock. He was no more than ten yards away and the gun in his right hand looked very big.

'Hold it right there,' said Lankton, 'and get off the rig one at a time. You first, fighting man.'

Daco climbed down, his mind racing. He figured Crants would be lurking somewhere near and had them covered. He and Lankton must have ridden straight on to Chisholm and taken the other road, as Dodds had said. When they reached this cut-off trail and seen no tracks, they'd known he hadn't passed the point yet, so they headed back along it to meet Dodds's rig.

Then it was Dodds's turn to get off the rig. As he put one foot on the ground, he turned slowly, but his concealed hand came up fast and the gun in it barked, loud as a cannon-shot in the silence. The shot went wide but the noise startled his horse which leaped forward, dragging the rig with it. As it started moving, Dodds tried to get back on, but it was moving too fast. He made a grab for Blackie's reins and managed to swing himself up into the saddle. Lankton dived off the trail to avoid being run over and by the time he was on his feet again, the rig, Blackie and Dodds were disappearing round the next bend in the road.

In the confusion Daco had sprinted a few yards off the trail to find cover. As he ducked down a bullet spanged off the rock just above his head: must be Crants. There was a second shot, a handgun, maybe Lankton shooting at Dodds or Dodds taking a pop back at Lankton. He heard the sound of the rig get faint, then there was silence and the night was left to three men and three guns.

Daco couldn't stay where he was. He knew he'd been spotted. Crouching as he went, he moved carefully from his rock to a stand of mesquite and from there to another rock. He risked a look over the top of it. Nothing moved. As he pondered his next move, he felt the barrel of a rifle dig into his back. He froze. A hand relieved him of his Colt.

'Over here. I got me a prisoner,' called a voice which Daco had last heard in Casey's boarding house.

For a big man, Crants had made no more noise than a cat.

'Move,' he said and dug the carbine hard into his back a second time. Daco moved.

The road where the ambush had happened was empty, save for Lankton.

'Which one have you got there?' he said.

When he saw Daco, he seemed disappointed.

'OK, since you're good at telling tales, you can tell me where Dodds is heading for. Make it fast, because I intend going after the son of a bitch.'

'He didn't say where he was going,' said Daco.

Lankton nodded and Crants smashed his fist into his right kidney. Daco gasped for breath and went down. Crants kicked him in the ribs three, four times, then stopped when Lankton held up his hand.

'Where'd he go?'

'Didn't say,' Daco gasped.

'Tie him up,' ordered Lankton, 'and soften him up some more.'

In the next few minutes, Daco took the biggest beating of his life. His arms were pinioned behind his back, so he couldn't ward off Crants's fists. Because his ankles were bound with rawhide, he could get no leverage to take avoiding action. More that once he felt consciousness about to go. But each time, Lankton called a halt, put the same question again and then, getting no answer that he liked, told Crants to start again. In the end, Daco felt himself falling into a dark hole.

'He ain't gonna come round, at least not for a long while,' said Crants, leaning over the prostrate body.

'Either he don't know or he wasn't telling,' said Lankton. 'Either way it don't matter none. Dodds is headed for

Pocaloca: there's nowhere else you can go on this trail. But I enjoyed asking Ward. It helped me get even.'

'Want me to finish him?' said Crants, reaching for his gun.

'No,' said Lankton with a smile. 'You roughed him up plenty hard. He's pretty close to being out of it already. If he does wake up, he'll be a lot more sore than I was after that lucky punch he caught me with. We'll leave him to enjoy it. Get the horses. Let's get after Dodds. We've wasted enough time already.'

Then they were gone.

5

Lost

Daco opened his eyes then shut them again, fast. The sun was up though not high yet, but high enough to be painful to look at. He turned his head away and tried again. His eyes were on a level with compacted sand and shale. Trails are regularly made of compacted sand and shale. He wondered why he was lying on a trail.

He tried to sit up. The effort made his head hurt first, then the rest of him, so he postponed the move. He tried to flex his arms, but somehow he couldn't. His legs didn't feel natural, they stayed stuck together. That had never happened before in the whole of his life. It was a puzzle. He gave up. He couldn't even work up enough interest to think about it. He floated off on his bed of sand and shale.

Later, he opened his eyes again. The sun was higher now, and it was hot, too hot to be lying in it. Instinct told him he needed to get into shade. His arms didn't work. His legs would bend but every movement they performed they performed together, as if they were tied up, trussed, like a chicken on a spit.

Trussed! Daco's eyes opened as memory returned.

He remembered the ambush, Dodds's getaway, Lankton asking the same question over and over, and Crants's boots, Crants's fists. With remembering came the knowledge that he was in a big fix.

He quelled the feeling of panic as it rose. He had been left here to fry on a trail that not many people used. The outlook was not good.

He shifted on to his side and tried to bend his arms. They were mighty sore but nothing seemed broken. He tried out his legs. They felt bruised but they worked fine too. His back hurt but he thought he'd live.

Forcing himself to pay no heed to the throbbing in his head, he craned his neck back as far as it would go and saw there was a rock by the side of the trail. It was a big rock and it threw a big shade. Gathering all his strength, he rolled over on his left side once, twice, then a third time, until he fetched up in the lee of the rock, sheltered from the burning sun.

Then he rested, waiting for the hurt to go away and his breathing to return to normal. In his time, he had faced grizzlies, swum icy rivers and gone up against men with big guns. Now he told himself he was going to have to do something really tough. He was going to have to sit up straight.

A couple of years rolled by while he waited for the right moment to come round. When it did he levered himself up on his elbows, dug his heels into the shale and pushed. Then he put all his weight on both fists and straightened his arms until he was sitting upright with his back against the rock. Strong men in fairs get applause and pennies thrown into their hats for doing less. He felt dizzy.

Some of the hurt was wearing off and his ideas were coming together. No use expecting a wagon or a friendly rider to pass by, he was on his own. He tried to make a mental list of what he had to do. He had to get water. But first he had to find it. Of course, in order to find it he'd need to walk. Before he could walk he'd need to get free. He wondered where he'd start at. In the end, he figured that getting free was top of the list.

He twisted his head left and right, looking for something he could use to saw through the rawhide Crants had used to tie him up with, an edge of rock or a sharp stone. If he could just free his legs, he could go looking further afield for something to work on the bonds holding his hands behind his back. But centuries of wind had worn the rock smooth and the shale was too fine to be of any use.

He was going to have to do it the hard way.

He pulled up his knees, bunched his hands and pressed his knuckles into the gravel. He raised his body and pushed backwards with his legs until he was sitting on his fists. His arms were now pressed close against his sides. He held his position for a few moments and took a few deep breaths. Then he widened his arms as far as they would go, yanked his fists forward and pushed hard again with his legs. Like men who spend long hours in the saddle, he was slim-hipped. But only a man as fit and agile as Daco Ward could have backed his hips through his arms without tearing a lot of muscles. Then he drew his knees up right under his chin and slowly worked his hands under them around his feet until they were resting on his shins and his head was on his knees.

Sweat ran down his face and dripped off his chin.

When the blood stopped pounding in his head he sat up and wiped the sweat with the inside of his shirtsleeves. Then with his right hand he leaned forward and picked at the knots at his ankles until his fingers were sore. But in the end, his legs were free and he stood up, stamping the ground to restore the circulation.

Though the sun was still high and blazing hot, he went out in it, scouting around for some way of cutting through the rawhide around his wrists. But the rocks were blown smooth by the winds and any that were broken crumbled as soon as he tried to work them. In the end, he knew he'd have to use his teeth. He went back to his rock and sat in the shade to do it. It took him an hour and left him with aching jaws.

While he worked, he sized up his situation.

It could be worse. He was in one piece and was on a trail, which was good. It meant there was a chance, however slim, that a wagon or a rider might show up at any time. It also stood to reason that if there were watering holes hereabouts they wouldn't be far off the trail.

And since it was a trail, it led to places. Pocaloca lay ahead, though how many days distant it was by foot he had no way of knowing. If he turned and took the trail back, the way he'd come, it was maybe twenty five miles to the turn-off to Chisholm, which was another forty. That made more than sixty-five miles in all. It was a daunting prospect but he reckoned he could do it. Especially since there'd be more likelihood of meeting up with somebody after the Chisholm turn-off.

Of course, he could save himself a lot of trekking by making straight across country to Chisholm, the direct way. But the risk was high. Apart from the distant hills of Pocaloca, the landscape was featureless. And where there's nothing to steer by, a man will get lost.

But however he looked at it, there was no denying he was in trouble. He was going to have to find water.

Lack of water was going to be a bigger problem than miles. The sun was still high, though it had begun to dip. It was maybe three in the afternoon and he hadn't had a drink for close on fifteen, sixteen hours. He slipped a pebble into his mouth and sucked on it. It helped.

He must have lost his hat when Crants got the drop on him. He went looking for it. He found the spot where he'd taken cover after jumping off Dodds's rig. His hat was lying on the ground where it had fallen. He picked it up, dusted it down and put it back on his head. He tried to remember the moment Crants had taken his gun. Had Crants stuck it in his belt? He'd have needed to keep both hands on his carbine, so maybe he'd just let it drop, or had he tossed it into a bush or behind a rock? Daco couldn't remember hearing it land anywhere but all the same he looked under bushes and behind rocks. His .44 had caught in the heart of a hand of sagebrush. It had come to no harm. He slipped it back into his holster. Doing that gave him a good feeling.

Then he climbed the biggest rock he could find and took his bearings. He rolled a cigarette and smoked it, though it dried his mouth.

The trail unwound through country littered with boulders and broken by low sandstone mesas. It came out of a jumble of boulders and disappeared into a pile of rocks further along. Ahead and both sides of the trail were unknown quantities. It was no contest. He decided to go back the way he'd come, but not until the heat had gone out of the day. Now that he'd made a decision, he felt better. He retreated into the shade, sat down again, tipped his hat low over his eyes and got what rest he could.

There came a moment when the big red sun at last slipped below the horizon. It was as if an oven door had suddenly been closed. The change woke

Daco. The rest had done him good but he was still sore. But he knew that walking would warm his muscles and massage the stiffness away.

He set off, heading north-east, walking steadily along the trail. The marks left by the wheels of Dodds's buckboard stood out sharply even in the twilight. He felt confident. He had a plan and he was putting it into operation. He had always kept himself in good physical shape and his aches and pains were falling away as he walked. But he didn't fool himself about the size of what he had to do.

He reckoned that if he kept up a steady pace, he'd make around three miles an hour. With rests, that meant he'd need ten hours or more just to make it back to the Chisholm turn off. He'd have to keep going most of the night if he was going to have any chance of surviving.

But even that proved beyond his reach. By midnight, he'd been walking for four hours and needed to rest. He'd held to the trail, which was mostly flat but from time to time rolled up and down ridges that he'd not felt when he'd ridden this way in pursuit of Dodds. But now they drained strength out of his legs. He forced himself to go on, for he knew he'd have to be out of the sun by around ten in the morning. At this time of the year, the temperature could reach 110° in the shade. He hoped there'd be shade when he needed it.

He walked on, putting one foot in front of the other. At first he thought some more about Lankton and wondered what his game really was. But after a while his thoughts started going round and round. They switched direction, settled on nothing for long, and eventually he told himself it would be fine for him to lie down a while. He found a stunted iron-wood tree, sat under it and rested. Then he told himself he'd feel stronger after a short nap.

He didn't see the soft grey dawn turn

crimson nor the sudden burst of sunrise. He woke when the sky was blue and the sun already up. Its rays warmed him, for the night had been cold. He sat up.

The land was still strewn with boulders and a light wind raised dust devils in the clear spaces between them. But hereabouts there were also reds and golds of cactus in flower and mists of purple sage. Then a quick movement caught his eye: a jack rabbit scampered across an open space. He also heard the sound of a mocking bird. His spirits rose. If animals and birds lived here, water could not be far away.

He lighted on a regular jack-rabbit trail. He followed it. He figured if lots of the critters came this way, it must lead to something important. Like water.

So it did. But he had to work hard to find it. He guessed it was maybe eleven o'clock by the time he found a muddy hole, a couple of feet across, with three or four inches of clear water at the bottom. He lay flat on his belly and scooped it out with his cupped hand. He drank his fill.

He selected a rock which threw solid shade and stretched out. He dozed for an hour. Then he went back to the water hole and drank some more. He sat down in his shade, pulled his gun from its holster and rested it on his leg, with his finger on the trigger.

The sun had already past its peak when a jack rabbit peered round the side of a rock, eyeing the water. Daco froze. When the critter was satisfied the coast was clear it hopped to the hole. It was about to take a drink when a bullet smashed through its brain.

Daco skinned and cleaned the rabbit. Then he made a fire and a spit and sat next to it, turning the carcass until it was ready.

When he'd eaten, Daco scooped a hollow for his hip in the sand and slept some more. He woke when the sun was low in the western sky.

He ate the rest of the jack rabbit and

drank again. He had nothing to carry water in, so he took on as much as he could. Then he hit the trail again.

He reckoned he'd covered a dozen miles the previous night. It wasn't enough. But he was feeling stronger now. There was a spring in his step and it lasted until the stars appeared. He took a rest. He perched on a rock because in the cooling night air he knew he would stiffen and it wouldn't be easy to get up again if he lay on the ground. Nor was he tempted to take his boots off to ease his swollen feet. If he did, he'd never get them back on.

In the dry, cloudless desert air, the sky was full of bright lights that twinkled down on him and made him feel that he was a very small item in a very big world. Then the moon came up and lit him royally on his way.

By three in the morning Daco had got very cold. Cresting a rise in the trail, he came across half a cart-wheel and a heap of broken buckboards, the remains of a rig that had come to grief.

He gathered up branches of sagebrush and used the wood to build a fire. He settled down beside it, to rest, to sleep. Using his hat for a pillow, he lay on his back and watched the stars.

He woke shivering. The fire was out and the sky was pigeon-grey. He stood up, dusted himself down, and set off again. As he walked he warmed up. It felt good to be on the move.

He reckoned he couldn't be more than a couple of hours from the Chisholm turn-off. But in the morning half-light, he lost the tracks of Dodds's rig on a stretch of the trail which was more shale than sand, and it was a good hour before he got back on the road again. By then, it was hotting up and he knew he'd have to find shade soon. And water. It was too early to stop yet.

Soon he had no choice. The sun was a dull brass ball in a lead sky and the heat was oppressive. Leaving the trail, he made for rock with an overhang and sat down in its shade. He was thirsty. He sucked a pebble. He sat watching and dozing and thinking of what he would do to Lankton and Crants when he caught up with them.

His eye caught a quick movement off to his left. In front of his hideaway was a stretch of flat, hard-baked sand. Moving across it and heading in his direction was a middling-sized rattler. Even desert rattlers can't stay out long in the noonday sun and this one was looking for a place to hide up. He'd sighted one: the rocks where Daco was holed out. It hadn't seen him but Daco sure didn't want that kind of company. He picked up a handful of shale and threw it.

The rattler stopped, head erect, flicking his tongue to get a scent. Then he came on. Daco wasn't in a sharing mood but he didn't want to waste a bullet if he could help it. He threw another fistful of shale. The rattler, head still up, went into a coil and glared. A dust devil sprang up and played round the snake before dying away. Daco lobbed a couple of larger rocks at him.

The rattler paused, then seemed to think better of it, uncoiled and crawled away. Daco watched him go. He counted maybe twelve joints on his rattle.

Though he kept watching, that was all the life Daco saw as the long morning wore into a longer afternoon. He dozed and woke, opening his eyes to the sting of the dried sweat that had grown a salty crust on his eyelids while he slept.

When it was about six o'clock he decided it was time to get back on the road. He had stiffened up again and he was hungry and thirsty. By starting now he'd have a couple of hours of light to look for water.

He looked but he didn't find.

He wished now that he'd shot the rattler. Snake can be good eating.

His swollen tongue moved like a lump of stiff shoe leather inside his dry mouth. Walking was harder now. He was tired and stumbled several times. Once he missed his footing and fell into a shallow depression that ran alongside the trail. It took a while to climb out and get moving again.

The moment came when he just had to stop and rest. But there was no wood for a fire now and the cold seemed more intense than ever. He found a patch of soft sand, lay down and shivered under the frigid light of the stars.

He must be only a mile or so from the Chisholm turn-off, but it might as well be a hundred. He'd got to the end of his strength. He wasn't going to make it. He thought of Lankton and Crants. He'd never settle his score now . . .

Then he felt himself being dragged from a great depth back into consciousness, through a sea of water, past waving plants which brushed over his face. Then he opened his eyes. The sun was up again but it was obscured by a black shape, a black muzzle, a muzzle that was nuzzling his mouth and cheeks and eyes.

It was Blackie!

6

Allies

As the buckboard swept past him, Dodds made a grab for Blackie's reins and swung himself up into the saddle. He lay flat on the stallion's neck and hung on for dear life. He heard shouts behind him, a shot and then silence. The ambush had been over in seconds. He had got away leaving Daco to the tender mercies of Lankton and Crants, who, though he hadn't seen him, wouldn't be far away.

He risked a look over his shoulder. He saw only the bend in the trail which the buckboard had taken at speed. Was that why the shooting had stopped? No one could shoot through rocks at a target they couldn't see.

The rig bucked as it flew along the road drawn by a horse that was still panicking. In contrast, Blackie was calm under his hand and running well within himself. If the rig continued to buck and swing the way it was, it would surely come to grief. Though it was making a fair speed, he reckoned he needed to be going faster than this if he was going to outrun Lankton and Crants. They weren't the sort to give up easy and they'd surely be coming after him.

At the same time, he wasn't intending to abandon the keg of gunpowder and the leather bag of samples he could see bouncing on the flatbed of the buck-board just feet from his nose.

He pulled a hunting knife from his belt, leaned forward and cut the rein that hitched Blackie to the back of the rig. Now he was free to take off fast if his pursuers got too close. But also he could stay near the rig and halt it when the horse pulling it either got tired or calmed down enough to be stopped.

Five minutes later he felt the buckboard begin to slow. Another five minutes and its speed had dropped further. Making the most of a wider stretch of trail, he overtook it, grabbed the draw-horse's reins and pulled the rig to a dead stop. The horse was blowing but had come to no hurt. He stopped and listened. There were no sounds of pursuit.

Dodds got off Daco's stallion and patted his own horse on the neck to calm it. He walked it on a space to settle it some more, then halted and hitched the reins around a point of rock. As he did so, he heard a snort at his back and turned. Blackie, who had been following quietly, had turned tail and was taking off. He cantered for fifty yards back along the trail they had ridden, then turned off it and started making across country. Dodds grinned. Stupid animal! he thought. It'll get itself lost and make bleached bones in the desert.

It was no loss and he turned to the job in hand. He had work to do and no time to waste. Anyways, he wasn't worried about not having a good mount. Hadn't Elmer Gamble remarked that the nag he rode was a superior piece of horseflesh, too good for pulling carts?

But it wouldn't take an Indian to read the tracks he had made and know he'd stopped here a while. It wasn't the place he needed for his purposes: he didn't want anyone to know his business.

He climbed aboard the rig and drove it on another mile before reining in at a stretch where his wheels left no trace in the shale. He got down and walked just twenty yards off the trail before finding what he was looking for: a flat patch of soft sand. Using his knife and hands, he scooped a shallow hole, then returned to the rig. He climbed aboard and manoeuvred the heavy keg to the back. He let down the tailgate and lowered the gunpowder to the ground. It was too heavy to carry, so he rolled it to the patch of sand and let it fall into the hole he had made. After covering it with sand, he snapped off a branch of sagebrush and wiped away all trace of his tracks.

After taking a long look at the lie of the land, so that he'd remember the place, he drove on for another mile and stopped again, making a lot of tracks this time. If anybody came looking for what he'd buried, they'd surely start here. But they'd find nothing.

He watered the horse and fed it. He filled his canteen from the water-cask on the rig and packed emergency rations in the sample bag, which he slung round his neck. He climbed a rock and took a look back.

In the morning twilight, he saw no riders coming after him.

Then he unharnessed the horse, just keeping reins and bit, and swung up on to its bare back.

He dug his bootheels into the horse's ribs and took off into the dawn, abandoning the buckboard which no longer hid any secrets.

★ ★ ★

'Get the horses,' said Lankton. 'Let's get after Dodds. We wasted enough time already.'

Leaving Daco trussed like a Thanksgiving turkey in the middle of the trail, they lit out in pursuit of Dodds.

At first they took it fast, but not so fast they'd miss the tracks left by the rig. If Dodds had turned off the trail, they wanted to know. He could be hid up in the rocks, waiting for them to gallop past.

The moon was low but soon the eastern sky began to turn milky, then ran through all the shades of red from purple through bright blood-red to delicate pink.

'Here, boss!' said Crants, reining in and staring down at the trail. 'He stopped here.'

Later: 'Looks like he walked the rig for a spell.'

Later: 'This is where Ward's big stallion took off back the way it come.'

They passed the spot where Dodds had buried the gunpowder without noticing a thing, not even the fresh-broken branch of sage from which he had cut his makeshift broom. Soon they came up with the abandoned buckboard.

'Where's that wooden barrel? And the samples?' raged Lankton. 'He couldn't have taken all that stuff on a horse. So he's got to have buried it. You take that side of the trail and I'll look over here.'

But though they searched long and hard, they found nothing.

By now the sun was up.

'What say we have something to eat,' said Crants. 'He left plenty stores on the rig.'

'Stow it,' barked Lankton. 'We ain't gone to all this trouble and ridden all this way to give up so easy. If we can't find the stuff, we'll have to find Dodds and make him tell us where it's at. And we ain't going to do that sitting here on our backsides filling our bellies.'

'Tell you what. We take what we need with us and we'll cook us up breakfast when we stop. We'll have to stop in an hour or so. Sun's getting hot. We can't afford to kill the horses. Dodds will stop too. No choice out here.'

It was a long speech from Crants. He paused, removed his hat and wiped the sweat off his forehead with his shirtsleeve.

'Maybe you're right,' said Lankton after a moment.

Crants grabbed what was left of the beef jerky and biscuit and refilled their canteens. He watered the horses from the cask, then knocked the lid off and tipped the cask on its side. The water seeped through the cracks in the rig's floor and vanished immediately into the sand.

'Don't want to be showing kindness to people as might be wanting to do us harm.' He grinned.

Lankton stared at him but said nothing.

They rode for close on two hours. They passed the turn-off for the direct road to Chisholm that they'd come along the previous day without meeting a soul or seeing any other tracks except those of Dodds's horse. Lankton would have gone further but Dodds's tracks petered out when the trail crossed flat rock.

'We'll pick him up later,' said Crants, 'now we know where he's headed. Only place he can go now is Pocaloca.'

They turned off the trail and made for a crop of heaped boulders that threw long, dark shadows against the bleached sand which shone white in the sun's rays.

Crants staked the horses so they wouldn't wander off, and broke out the provisions. Then the two men slept.

When they woke, the sun was past its zenith. But it was still too hot to travel.

Crants broke out the rest of the supplies. As they ate, he said:

'You reckon Dodds is on the level? Way I figure, he's too smart to be as dumb as he acts.'

'I ain't worked out what his game is, but there's more to him than meets the

101

eye. The feller in the assay office said them gold nuggets he brought in were the genuine article. Same went for the sample of ore: high grade, three or four dollars the ton guaranteed. Trouble is, he never saw gold as good that come out of any mine or level in the county, nor that quality of ore neither. He said Dodds told him it all came from up Pocaloca way. According to the assay clerk, the rocks up there are all wrong for it. He never heard of anyone making a strike in that neck of the woods.'

'Way I see it, it don't much matter where it came from as long as I get me a piece of it,' said Crants with a leer.

'The other thing the assay officer said was that Dodds never filed a claim. Don't make sense. What is Dodds up to?'

His question vanished without answer into the heat-filled silence.

Then the stillness was broken by a faint sound that was like a match being scraped on rock. A smell of tobacco reached the two men where they sat in their shade. Then a voice said:

'And I never beat you fair and square at the poker table neither. I'd been bottom-dealing all day and had cards in most pockets except the one Crants slipped a couple into. If the dude with the fancy fists hadn't rumbled you, I guess I'd have been caught red-handed, seeing as I was guilty as charged.'

'Dodds!' breathed Crants. 'Where'n tarnation he come from?'

'Blast his eyes!' cursed Lankton. 'I knew he didn't beat me fair and square.'

He got up and peered carefully round the edge of the rocks that had given them shade. Nothing stirred.

'What you want, Dodds?' barked Lankton. 'What's your game?'

'This ain't no game. We need to parley. I got a proposition.'

'Where's he at?' whispered Crants. 'I cain't rightly tell the direction his voice is coming from. But the wind is bringing his smoke this way and that puts him behind the wolf rock yonder.'

He had his gun out and pointed with it to a boulder that had the shape of a wolf's head.

Lankton nodded: 'That's where I put him too. Ed, circle round, come up at his back, get the drop on him. But don't kill him. I want him alive so he can come clean about the gold and the rest of it.'

Crants said nothing but slipped away, using the rocks as cover and keeping the outcrop where they'd sheltered between him and the wolf head boulder.

'You want to parley or what?' came Dodds's voice.

'I'm thinking about it. Tell me what there's to parley about,' replied Lankton, playing for time to allow Crants to get round back of him.

As he spoke, he climbed up the rock and risked a look over the top. He had a good sight of the wolf boulder. There was no sign of Dodds.

'I told you. I got a proposition.'

'What sort of proposition?'

The answer was a bullet that whipped the hat off his head. Lankton ducked back down behind his rock.

'Don't mess with me, Lankton,' said Dodds, and there was menace in his voice.

Crants listened to the voices as he worked his way round to get behind his target. He could have sworn Dodds's voice kept on coming from the same place but every time he thought he'd just peek over one more rock and he'd see him clear as day he'd find nothing. Dodds must be keeping on the move.

He took a look round one more rock and found himself staring down the barrel of Dodds's rifle.

He started back, reaching for his gun, but Dodds was too quick for him. Crants got the bullet straight in the forehead. A look of surprise crossed his face which suddenly went blank as life went out of him and he collapsed like a puppet that's had its strings cut.

'I said no messing, Lankton,' called

Dodds while the sound of the shot was still dying away. 'I say that sending your man out after me ain't a friendly act. But he won't trouble anybody again.'

While Lankton was still wondering if this meant what he thought it did, he saw a hat tossed from behind a rock way to his left, maybe twenty yards from wolf-head rock. The hat hit the ground, rolled a few turns on its brim and settled in the sand.

'He won't need his hat neither,' said Dodds, 'seeing that he ain't got all his head to set it on.'

Dodds had shot Crants! Lankton couldn't believe it. Yet there was the hat to prove it.

'We got us a stalemate,' came Dodds's voice. 'We could sit here like this for a week and still be no further on. Way I see it, we only got one way round it, and that's for you to throw your gun where I can see it and then come out after it.'

'So you can gun me down? No thanks!'

'I don't want to kill you, Lankton. Did you forget already? I told you, I got a proposition for you. I ain't going to shoot a man I got plans for.'

Lankton thought it over. With Crants dead, he felt exposed. Ed had been a good man, tough and fast with a gun. Dodds was clearly better, foxier, faster, tougher, so it wouldn't be easy to put him away. He thought awhile, took out his makings and rolled two smokes.

'Well?' called Dodds. 'You coming, or do I have to come and get you?'

'What's this proposition you keep talking about?'

'That's better. There's money in it. You'll like it when you hear what I got to say. So how about it? We can talk easier if we're face to face.'

Lankton's answer was his revolver tossed on to the sand to his left of the boulder he was using as cover.

'That's good,' called Dodds. 'Now you come out with your hands in the air.'

Lankton stepped out of the shade

with his hands up, holding the two smokes. It was not as hot now, for the sun was low in the sky. It shone directly into his eyes and was still strong enough to blind him. But it wouldn't have made any difference. Dodds was on him before he was aware of what was happening. He felt the gun in his back and the hand that frisked him found no gun but took away his knife. Then the barrel was gone from his spine.

'OK, you can turn round now.'

Lankton lowered his arms. Dodds had put his gun up and was now standing in front of him as easy as if he were a preacher saying hello to a favourite member of his flock. He had Lankton's gun stuck in his belt.

'If we're going to talk, we'd be better in the shade. Sun's a trial even though it's run its course for today.'

'We'll talk,' said Lankton, relaxing as he walked into the nearest shade. 'Smoke?'

Dodds took one of the cigarettes in Lankton's fist, lit it, then held out the rest of the match to Lankton's hand-rolled.

'You said you got plans for me. What plans might they be?'

'Golden plans,' said Dodds, perching on a rock. As he sat, he pulled Lankton's gun from his belt. 'Here. Better have this back if it helps you to trust me. Evens things up.'

He settled back, drew on his cigarette and explained:

'Ever been out Pocaloca way? No? You ain't missed much. One-horse town. Half-assed farmers and sheep-men mostly. Ain't nothing there. But a few years back there was a prospector, name of Raymond Tuke, hit a silver vein. It paid fair for a while and he got to the end of it. He never found any more.

'Now old Raymond was a man with a way with words. You know what he called his claim up in the mountains back of Pocaloca? He called it Silveroo. More in hopes than in what his strike was worth. But the name stuck

109

somehow. There's even a homestead up there still calls itself that.'

'Interesting tale, Dodds, but where's it taking us?'

'When I was up sniffing around Silveroo, I hit the golden jackpot!'

'Gold? But you said there wasn't any gold, only silver — and not much of that.'

'Lankton, you must know there's gold and gold. The kind you grub out of the rock is the hard-earned sort. But the kind to have is the variety that folds and sits comfortably in a man's wallet.'

'That I can see. But what's this to do with Silveroo and you and me?'

'I told you. When I was in Clayton Creek I had the assay office check out a few samples I said came from the old Silveroo diggings.'

'What samples?'

'Small nuggets, lumps of ore. Gold.'

'You salted Silveroo with gold?'

'Would be a liar if I said no. When word gets around, and you can't keep a strike secret for long, there'll be a rush.

There always is. Picture the scene. We're sitting on a gold mine. First man comes along with the right price gets to buy it. Then off we go, with his folding money in our wallets.'

'It won't work,' said Lankton sceptically.

'Ain't the first time I done it,' said Dodds. 'It don't pay fortunes but it's a lot safer than robbing banks and it sure beats working for a living. You take the money and are gone before the new owner gets wise to that fact that he's been gypped.'

Lankton looked at him with renewed interest. Then he frowned:

'If you've done it before, how come you need me?'

'Nobody's been near Silveroo for thirty years or so. There's ocotillo and scrub sprung up all over it. It sure as heck don't look like a claim that's being worked. It'll need some titivating, make it look the part. There's got to be a likely-looking shaft and a heap of likely-looking spoil, the sort that comes from real gold workings. The hole we can make easy. But we'll have to haul the spoil from worked-out claims I know down in Jade County. It'll take a bigger cart than the buckboard and a team to haul it. I can't do all the work myself, I got to have help. But mostly I need somebody to watch my back. Pity about your friend. He was a neat mover for such a big man.'

'Sure was, but Ed wasn't fast enough to take you. Let's just say he flunked the test.'

Dodds looked Lankton in the eye, held it for a moment, and then went on:

'I had a partner but he flunked the test too. I thought Daco Ward was my man. He can look after himself and thinks on his feet. But there's two things wrong with him. First he's too smart, second he's as straight as a road that has no turning. I cain't abide people who are honest. They make me nervous. Maybe it's all on account of having a preacher for a grandfather. But a man that's law-abiding rubs me up the wrong way. Being good gets in the way of business. But, praise the Lord, there ain't no God this side of the Missouri and that suits me just fine.'

'Spare me the life story, Dodds. I heard it before. Life stories are all the same, and the ending is always 'poor me'. You said something about a proposition. What you putting on the table?'

'I do the thinking and talking, you ride shotgun and take charge of the spadework. I'll help with that, of course. With my regular partner, rest his soul, I used to split sixty-five to thirty-five in my favour. On this one, seeing as how I've done all the work so far and laid out cash for the samples and the gunpowder — '

'Gunpowder!'

'We'll come to that part in a while. Anyway, since I was the one who found Silveroo, salted the mine, put the word about and spent good money on supplies, I reckon a two-way divide of eighty-five to fifteen would be fair.

When the job's done, we move on and do it again some place else, and the next time around it'll be the two thirds/one third arrangement I had with Tom.'

'Make it eighty to twenty and it's a deal,' said Lankton.

Dodds thought a moment, then he smiled.

'Done,' he said, and held out his hand. 'We start now. We got two things to do. We got to go out and get ourselves a wagon and team. But first, since it's cooled off enough now, we got a little job to do. So come on, we're going prospecting for gunpowder. And I know the very place where we'll strike lucky, though luck don't come into it!'

7

Partners

Blackie stopped nuzzling him the moment Daco moved and then backed off a few steps and waited. Daco staggered to his feet, clung to the stallion's neck for support and reached for the canteen of water which hung from his saddle. It was three-quarters full. He could have drunk a river dry, but he knew better than to go hard at it. He took it slow. He wet his lips, paused, swallowed a mouthful and then another, savouring the moment. It was warm but he had never realized how good water tasted.

When he felt life flowing through his parched veins, Daco reslung the canteen over his pommel and checked Blackie for injuries. He had come to no visible harm and walked on happily enough when Daco swung up into the saddle and rode him into the shady lee of a large outcrop of rocks. Judging by the sun's elevation, it was not much past midday and too soon to be going on his way. Anyway, he was feeling about as lively as a dead gopher. He dismounted, took the saddle off Blackie's back, and hitched him to a stand of sagebrush which he started grazing.

When the heat eased, Daco, feeling rested, drank some more of his water, resaddled the stallion and moved off along the still empty road. As day turned to dusk, Blackie scented water in a hole just off the trail and they stopped to drink. The moon came up and by midnight they were at the Chisholm turn off. Daco could have stopped but he and his horse were fresh enough to continue on to the town, which they reached after sun-up.

Daco saw that Blackie was fed and watered and looked after in the stables of the Lucky Penny saloon before he got himself a room. He didn't feel hungry, probably too tired. But he ordered a pint jug of coffee, took it up to his room, set it down on the table by his bed, dropped on to the mattress and was asleep before he could pour himself a cup.

When he woke, the coffee was long cold, but he drank it all the same. Then, feeling hungrier than he had since he was a fast-growing boy, he went looking for breakfast, though it was now four in the afternoon.

Chisholm was smaller than Clayton. The main street had a barber's shop, a general stores, a bank, the Lucky Penny saloon and Ma Kennedy's eating-house. Ma Kennedy was no great shakes as a cook but Daco ate the pork and beans and the coffee she set before him with relish. When he'd done, he leaned back on two legs of his chair and rolled a cigarette which he smoked slowly.

Through the window he watched the bustle of Chisholm's main and only street.

'Now there's an odd thing,' said Ma
Kennedy, when she came to clear his
table. 'Bank's got its blinds down.
Looks like they closed early. Never did
see that before. Old Mr Robson is a
man you can set your watch by.' Then
off she went, back to her kitchen to
cook up more chancy stews. Daco
made a note to eat his next meal
someplace else.

Robson's Bank was directly across
the street. Like Ma said, the blinds of
the ground-floor windows were down
and no one was going in or coming out.
Hitched at the rail were three horses
and there were a couple of buggies
tethered there too. At first Daco paid
no attention. But then he wondered
why so much horseflesh was kicking its
heels outside a bank that was closed for
business. He looked again and dropped
his chair on to four legs in surprise. The
second horse from the steps leading up
to the bank looked familiar, and he
knew why. The last time he'd seen it
had been pulling Dodds's buckboard.

He checked his gun and stepped out into the street.

The sun shone straight on the bank's frontage. Nothing seemed amiss. The townsfolk of Chisholm were going about their business as usual.

Daco crossed the street, walked up the steps and tried the door to the bank. It was locked. He rattled the knob and knocked. He kept knocking and asking 'Anybody home?'

A few passers-by stopped to look, then walked on with puzzled expressions on their faces.

Daco didn't give up his knocking, saying he had urgent business and how it was too early for the bank to close. When it was clear he wasn't going to give up easily, there was the sound of a key turning in the lock and the door swung open. Inside, he saw two bank tellers behind their counters and maybe half a dozen customers. They didn't look natural. They stood as if they had been posed by an artist to play the parts of ordinary folk doing ordinary things. But

they just looked stiff and scared. Daco
stepped inside, knowing what he'd find.

The door slammed shut behind him
and the key turned again in the lock. A
hand reached from behind and relieved
him of his gun. Daco tried a back elbow
which found a target and brought an
audible gasp. He swung round and
found himself looking down the barrel
of Tucker Lankton's Colt. Tucker wore
his kerchief over his nose but there was
no mistaking the build, the voice, the
strut. Tucker had ridden the blow and
was still in charge.

'Well now, look who we've got here,'
he said, then called out: 'Come here!
You got to see this!'

As he tossed Daco's gun into a
corner a door to a room behind of the
counter opened and Dodds, also with
his face masked, stepped through it. He
had a gun in his hand too, only his gun
was pointing back into the room at a
target Daco couldn't see.

'So you used up another of your nine
lives, Daco,' he said. 'How many you

got left now? I got this feeling you're about to find out you ain't got none left at all. You just ran out of lives.'

He thought a moment, then he said: 'Tie him up and gag him.'

Daco read the situation at once. Dodds and Lankton didn't want any shooting, not until they'd opened the safe and filled their bag with banknotes ready for a fast getaway. Just one shot would rouse the town, maybe bring the law, if there *was* a lawman in Chisholm. But even if there wasn't, it would attract attention they didn't want.

Dodds went back into the manager's office. From it came the thick sounds of fist on flesh and cries of pain from what sounded like an old man. It was Robson defending his business. He wouldn't hold out much longer, not if he went on taking that sort of beating.

'You,' Lankton called to a burly, grizzled man, aged fifty or so, who had been waiting his turn when the bank had been raided, 'take this rope and tie him up.'

And he pushed Daco into the middle of the room and kicked the legs from under him. As he fell, Daco twisted, turned and lashed out with his right foot. The heel of his boot caught Lankton on the knee. He howled with pain but he didn't go down. But the barrel of his gun did and Daco used the moment to get on his feet and land a sweet right on his jaw. Lankton staggered back, but kept hold of his gun which he raised and pointed at Daco's head.

'Go on, Lankton, pull the trigger. But if you shoot, you'll bring the law running and you'll never get away.'

'Ain't no law in Chisholm except old Gabe Stukely and he ain't fired a gun since George Washington was a boy.'

'Got your orders, haven't you. Smart boy Dodds got you where he wants you? And there was me thinking that you was the clever one.'

Before he could test his theory that the last thing the robbers wanted was to draw attention, Dodds's voice cut in behind him:

'He cracked. Opened the safe. Money's in the bag. Time to go.'

Lankton, still covering Daco, backed to the door, felt for the key behind him and turned it.

At that moment, there was a gunshot. It came from the door to the manager's office. Old man Robson stood leaning against the jamb with a venerable pistol that might have seen service in the War of Independence two generations ago. It was a big bore piece and fired a single shot before it needed reloading. The bullet went wide and made a hole as big as a man's fist in the wall. The recoil spun him back into the room, so when Dodds turned and fired from the hip the shot gouged a lump out of the doorjamb but did no other damage.

But the diversion gave Daco time to smash Lankton's hand down and land another punch on his jaw. The gun hit the floor. As Daco bent down to pick it up Dodds, with the leather bag slung over one shoulder and his gun in his right fist, used his left to grab the nearest customer, an elderly woman. He held her in front of him, an arm around her neck, like a shield.

'Back off, Daco, or the old girl gets it. Drop the gun and go stand behind the counter. The rest of you, lie down on the floor.'

Daco did as he was told. The frightened customers all lay down on the floor.

'Tucker, pick up your shooter and don't lose it again. Take a look outside and see if that shot got anybody all fired up.'

Lankton opened the door a few inches and looked out.

'There's a few women and old timers looking this way, but none of them got guns. Seems like it's all clear.'

Dodds moved slowly towards the door, keeping the old lady between himself and the counter behind which Daco and the two tellers were standing. When he reached the door, he told Lankton to give him the key to the bank door and get on his horse with the money bag. Then he backed out of the bank and, after pushing the old lady inside, loosed off a shot at Daco. Then he slammed the door shut and locked it.

The bullet missed its target and zipped away to his left. Daco leaped over the counter and retrieved his gun. But by the time he reached the window and flipped the blind up, the two riders were fifty yards down the street, galloping hard, scattering pedestrians and raising a cloud of dust. Then they disappeared round a bend before Daco could get a single shot at them.

Daco swore in frustration. With the butt of his gun he smashed the window and climbed out. The people who'd been watching from across the street emerged from wherever they'd taken cover when the shooting started. Daco unlocked the door with the key that was still in it. Inside, he saw one of the bank's customers lying on the ground, with blood oozing from his left arm. Daco shouted to the onlookers to get a doctor because there was a man down. The old lady was badly shaken but was otherwise unharmed. One of the tellers was tending to old Mr Robson who'd taken a savage beating. He needed medical attention too.

Meanwhile the customers who had been held prisoner had got to their feet. They all looked pale and shaken, but otherwise had got off lightly. The big-made, grizzled man who had a bullet in the arm was not badly hurt and seemed to be taking the whole episode in his stride.

'Nice try, young feller,' he told Daco. 'You did what you could but none of it come out right. Mack Macdonald is the name. A pleasure to know you, sir.'

Daco took charge, reassuring the ladies and directing the bank staff to start clearing up the mess. Then he accompanied Macdonald who, despite his protests, was stretchered back to the Lucky Penny where he said he had a room for the night. But he refused to be taken upstairs, ordered whiskey and sat at a table in the saloon. He told the barkeep to bring the bottle and sat himself down opposite Daco.

'It's been a costly afternoon for me, Daco. Daco is what those bad guys called you, isn't it?'

'Daco Ward's the name, Mr Macdonald.'

'Mack. My friends call me Mack. Well, Daco, I was about to deposit a bag of cash but they bust in and took it before it even crossed the counter. I won't be ruined but it's a big hit and I don't aim to take it lying down. Still, I won't be doing much about it for a while, not with this arm.'

Doc Parks bustled in. He said old man Robson would live, no question, but he wouldn't be coming into the bank for a spell, though, knowing how stubborn the old fool was, you never could tell. Then he turned to the gunshot patient who, he'd been told, was holed up in the saloon. He would fix him up then and there, unless he wanted to go upstairs and be private.

Macdonald said he'd be fine where he was. The doc pulled away the kerchief Daco had tied round his arm to stanch the bleeding, cut his shirt-sleeve and peered at the wound.

'Looks like the bullet might have just nicked the bone. But it passed through, so no need for me to go excavating for lead. I'll just clean and bind it.'

The doc worked fast. He clamped a cloth over the wound until the bleeding slowed. Then he grabbed the whiskey bottle by the neck and splashed a good snort over it. Macdonald gritted his teeth until the pain eased and said it was a waste of good booze. Doc Parks bound his arm with a fresh bandage, pulled his neckerchief off and used it to make a sling for Macdonald's arm. Then he stood up.

'That should do the trick. But you'll have to keep that arm still. Until I tell you different, you drink your whiskey with your left hand. Got to go now, Mrs McTaverty is due any minute. I got five dollars on it says it's a boy.'

Then he was gone.

Macdonald said Daco was to pour more whiskey and, if he had the time, stay and talk for a while. Since Dodds and Lankton were long gone, there wasn't much Daco could do. Anyways, Macdonald had stopped a shot that had been intended for him. So he settled back in his chair and listened while Mack explained how he came to be unlucky enough to be at the bank at the exact moment that the two masked men rushed in.

'I got me a claim down in Jade County. There's just me works it and my partner, a good man, Ned Thomson. I rode up from there to cash in our goods through the assay office here. Six months' work. Got the gold weighed and valued and paid for in honest dollar bills. I was about to hand the cash over the counter when those thieving hogs walked in and started waving guns around. Wasn't nothing I could do. They stole the money and with it half a year of my life. They could also have killed me. I ain't going to forget it. Now they're gone and I don't know where to start. But any fool could tell they knew you and that you knew them. So maybe you could give me a lead?'

'Four, mebbe five days ago was the first time I set eyes on either of 'em,' began Daco. It seemed a real long time. Then he told Macdonald all he knew.

★ ★ ★

Bill Dodds and Tucker Lankton rode hard along the Pocaloca road until their horses were lathered. The moon was well up when they turned off the trail, covered their tracks, and holed up after making half a mile through the boulder-littered landscape. They lit a fire in the lee of a rock, where it wouldn't be seen, brewed coffee and ate some of the beef jerky and biscuit Lankton had taken from Dodd's abandoned buckboard.

'Want to know how much we got away with?' asked Dodds. 'Build up the fire so I have more light and I'll count it.'

'That can wait. First I want to know if you plugged Daco for good. He recognized us! So he can tell the law who we are — '

'Tell old Stukely? What's the sheriff going to do? Shake his walking-stick at us?'

'He could call in the US marshal. And the marshal would get a posse together and see to it our description was posted up all over the county. We'd be fair game for any bounty hunter who reads Wanted notices. Or the bank could do it, without waiting for no marshal. But if Daco's dead, he's not going to tell nobody nothing.'

'Relax, Tucker. There's not going to be a posse and there'll be no Wanted notices neither. We robbed a bank is all. Happens every day. If they started putting up notices for every bank robber in this state, there wouldn't be enough walls to put them on. I don't know if I stopped Daco for good. I didn't have much time to get a real shot. But even if he does come after us, we can handle him. So, just forget it and get that wood like I asked you.'

When the fire was burning bright, Dodds counted the money. Then he leaned back against the rock, lit a cigarette and breathed the smoke down contentedly.

'Remember I told you salting claims was easier work than robbing banks? Well, I was wrong. We got three thousand dollars here and it took us a couple of hours. We'd be going it some to get as much for a claim we'd spent a month salting, not to mention the expense involved.'

'That's fifteen hundred apiece. What are you going to do with your half?'

'What we, the two of us, are going to do with the money is what we planned. We're going to buy ourselves a wagon and we're going to salt that claim. The rest we split.'

'But who gets to carry the three thousand? You and me and money don't go back a long way, but so far it hasn't been an easy ride.'

'If that's how you want it, we'll split it now.'

Dodds riffled through the notes.

'There's your share — go on, count it to be sure — and this is mine. When we have to lay out money for expenses, we each come up with half. So don't spend it all.'

'On what?' said Lankton, with a laugh. 'Look around you, do you see saloons and card-tables and girls? I don't.'

'Get some rest, Tucker. We got work to do tomorrow. We got a trip to make down to Jade County and a wagon to buy so we can haul that load of spoil.'

The night was still warm. Dodds stretched out on his back and, using his bedroll for a pillow, was soon asleep.

Tucker Lankton, on the other side of the fire, lay on his side. While the flames died leaving only the red glow of embers, he watched Dodds as he slept.

Or was he sleeping?

He kept one hand on the wallet in which he had put his share of the proceeds from the robbery.

He kept the other on his gun.

He did not sleep until the night sky began to turn pale.

8

Trouble At Burton Gulch

Mack had planned to get straight back to Jade County without spending any more time in Chisholm than he had to, split the money with his partner, Ned Thomson, then resume work on their claim. But his shot-up arm put paid to that idea just as it did to his determination to set off in pursuit of the two men who had stolen six months' work.

Daco had been surprised to see Dodds with Lankton, for the last time he'd seen Dodds he had been looking down the barrel of Lankton's gun. Nor could he figure out what Lankton was doing without Crants to back him up. He had them down for long-time partners. If they'd gone their separate ways there must have been a good reason for it. If they hadn't, then there were three men to deal with, not two, with Crants holed up someplace out of town.

He had plenty of evidence that said they made a bad pair, but that was all. He didn't know where they hailed from, whether they'd been passing through Clayton and were just picking up some spending money working the cards in the Silver Slipper while they waited for a train out, or whether they had dealings or connections in town or lived somewhere in Box Tree County. But Dodds was different. He knew nothing about the man except what he himself had admitted to. And given the shifty way he had behaved, nothing he'd said could be considered trustworthy.

Mack threw more doubts on his bona fides. He was interested in Dodds's account of his strike up Pocaloca way.

'I spent a couple of months up there once,' he said, 'but more around Silveroo than in Pocaloca itself. I didn't see any gold and I never ran across any book-learned man name of Dodds neither, nor any family of that name. Still, it's a big, spread-out sort of place, with more mountains up there than people. So mebbe we never rode the same trails on the same days. It happens. But you'd have thought I'd have heard tell of a surveyor. A man who knows about rocks draws prospectors like bees to a honeypot. Nor did I get to hear about a sheepman with an operation of any size up there, though it's grass country, they get a lot of rain. It's the mountains. They pull every last drop out of the clouds before they ever get to the plain, which is why this neck of the woods is so durned hot and dry. You said he had a sister?'

'That's what he said. Name of Annie.'

'Since we got nothing else to go on, Pocaloca's as good a place to start with as any. We'll go pay a call on Annie. When, that is,' said Mack, 'I'm up to the mark and if you want to come. You're quite a hero in town and there's talk of offering you old Gabe Stukely's job as sheriff. He says he'd be glad to step down.'

Daco thought about it.

He had no hankering to wear a star on his vest, and there wasn't anything to keep him in Chisholm. Add to that the fact that Mack's stolen money was none of his concern. But again, there was nothing calling him any place in particular. And though what Mack did next was his own affair, Daco didn't like the feeling that he'd been made a fool of by Dodds, nor could he forget that Lankton and Crants had left him in the desert to die. A man shouldn't walk away from those things. There was a score to be settled. When it came down to it, he had no choice. He threw in his hand with Mack.

Besides, he liked him. There was something straightforward and honest about the man.

When Doc Parks came the next day to see how his patient was faring and change the dressing, he said the swelling was down, which meant the bullet hadn't nicked the bone.

'So it's just a flesh wound you got there. You were lucky. Keep it clean and keep it still and you'll be fine. By the way, I lost my five bucks: it was a girl.'

When he'd gone, Mack said:

'This puts me in a fix. I need to get news back to Ned, tell him about the robbery to make sure he don't get the idea I ran out on him.'

'How far is this Jade County?'

If Daco was to follow up the Pocaloca lead, he'd need Mack and his prospecting know-how with him. But since it looked like Mack was going to have to stay in Chisholm, he said he'd ride down and tell Ned.

Burton Gulch, Jade County, was half a day's ride south through the same arid terrain where he'd been left to die. A sign to Burton Gulch directed him off the trail which led him up into the mountains where the temperature dropped quickly as he gained height and there was enough rainfall to support green-leaved bushes and even trees. Burton Gulch was a shallow valley with a stream at the bottom, which led upwards in a series of rocky ledges.

When he got there, he stopped off at a single-storey clapboard building. A painted board swinging on rusty chains declared it to be Frenchie's General Store.

A number of men were hanging around outside, exchanging news and having a laugh. Miners round about got their supplies and provisions from Frenchie Petitloup rather than waste a whole day trekking all the way to Chisholm and back. Frenchie sold everything from thread to coffins. Inside was a bar made of rough planks laid across barrels.

Daco went in, bought a drink and asked where he'd find Ned Thomson. He was directed to a trail which followed the stream up the valley. After a while he found the claim Mack had told him about. Ned, a wiry man of forty, with a drooping moustache, a red-checked shirt and denim pants tucked into old calf-length army boots, was sitting on an upturned box talking to two or three men who worked a claim a little way up the valley from theirs.

Daco introduced himself and sat himself down. He drank the whiskey Ned poured for him, then took him aside and explained what had happened.

'Is Mack OK?' was the first thing Ned asked.

His next thought was to light out of Burton Gulch and go after the men who had robbed him and his partner.

'I'll get my gun,' he said. He was all fired up.

'Mack said no. He said somebody's got to stay with the claim. You can't just leave a claim to look after itself and expect no harm will come to it.'

'Well, you can stay,' said Ned, 'I'm going.'

'It ain't mine to care for,' said Daco,

'anyway, Mack and me, we saw them and you didn't. So we're the ones who get to go.'

In the end, Daco made Ned see it his way.

By this time the sun was well down. It was too late for Daco to head back to Chisholm and he accepted Ned's invitation to share his dinner and stay the night. When they'd eaten they walked down to Frenchie's stores for a drink. The dusk was gathering, but there was more than enough light for there to be no mistake. Just off the trail, maybe twenty yards short of the stores, sitting on a high-sided wagon drawn by two powerful draught horses, were two men whom, though they now wore their kerchiefs round their necks and not over their faces, Daco recognized at once.

He stopped, turned away and whispered urgently in Ned's ear.

'See those two fellers on the heavy rig there? Take a peek but don't stare.'

Ned looked up.

'What about them?' he said.

'They're the fellers who robbed the bank and stole your money. I said don't stare. And don't do anything hasty. They're a real mean pair of coyotes.'

'I ain't aiming to go up to them and ask for our money back,' said Ned. 'But if you don't have a notion of doing something about it pronto, I'll figure something out myself.'

'Stow it. You ain't even wearing a gun.'

Daco thought hard. There wasn't much going for them — they were a couple of amateurs up against two professionals — but he sure wasn't going to lose the element of surprise.

'That's Chuck Olson's rig,' said Ned. 'How did they get their hands on it?'

'Couldn't say. Best way is to ask him. Come on. It don't look like Dodds and friend are planning to go far tonight. The light's almost gone. They'll bed down and move out tomorrow. Come on, let's see what Chuck's got to say.'

They climbed back up the rough

track for maybe a quarter of a mile, passing Ned and Mack's claim, and stopped at Chuck Olson's camp. Olson was a big, friendly Swede and he was just finishing his evening meal. Choosing his questions carefully so as not to give anything away, Daco learned that two men had come by earlier that day, said they'd seen his rig, that it was just what they needed for a big haulage job they'd landed, and how much did he want for it and the horses. They had cash — *'course they did*, thought Daco, *most of it the bank's and the rest Mack's* — and didn't even try to beat down the price but just stumped up, no questions asked.

'Looked like town dudes to me, still wet behind the ears,' said Chuck. 'Didn't seem to know the price of things. Big spending fellers. They paid over the odds. I said they could look round and see if there was anything else they wanted. At those prices I wouldn't have refused them anything. But they said no, just the rig and pair. Then they harnessed up and drove down the hill. Last I seen of them.'

'You sure they're bank-robbers?' Ned asked Daco, as they left Chuck Olson's campfire and headed back down the valley. 'First time I heard of outlaws who went round paying for stuff they could steal for nothing.'

'They don't want trouble is why. I don't know what they're up to, but they ain't keen to draw more attention to themselves than they can help.'

'Fair enough. So now we need to find out what they're planning.'

'For that we'll have to get close to them,' said Daco.

'Come on then. Hiding away up here ain't going to get the job done,' said Ned who, still fired up, led the way back down to the store.

They stopped off at the claim and strapped on their gunbelts. By this time, it was nearly dark and the wind was rising.

Although it was late, the store was well lit. Three or four lamps suspended

145

from the overhang burned over a knot of men who were still there, though they weren't buying bacon and shovels now but drinking Frenchie's home-distilled rot-gut hooch which he sold for eighty cents a gallon.

Keeping out of the circle of light, Daco and Ned scrutinized the raucous group for the two strangers. They weren't there. But the wagon hadn't moved from where they had last seen it, twenty yards off the trail, under a tree. The dark was intense now but voices could be heard coming from the wagon, for the two men had settled down on the flatbed for the night.

After a brief, whispered confab it was decided that Daco would get round back of the wagon, where the cover was thick and he'd be able to get real close. Ned burrowed into a stand of sage-brush. There he had the wind in his face. It blew the men's voices away from Daco but towards Ned.

He could make out some parts of what the two men were saying very clearly, but others not at all, for as it gusted the wind snatched their words away and dispatched them unheard into the night. One voice said he'd go over the plan. At first light, they'd drive the wagon up the valley, find a worked-out claim and make up a load of spoil. Not just any kind of spoil. It had to have a good leavening of quartz and slate in it. Then they'd take off. They'd go back to 'galshaders'. Ned couldn't work out what this was. A river? A mountain? A town? Then Ned heard another word he didn't understand. It came to him muffled and fuzzy: 'sillero'.

The wind was getting stronger and blowing the words right past his ears. He got slowly to his feet, crouched to make himself small and moved closer to the wagon so that he could hear better. He'd made four or five yards when his right boot caught a fallen branch. The dead wood snapped with a crack that rose above the rush of the wind. He dropped flat on his stomach. As he did so, the moon, which had been hidden by clouds, was suddenly unveiled and lassoed him with a noose of light. He froze.

The voices stopped in mid-sentence. Ned knew he was in trouble.

'Somebody out there,' said the voice.

At that moment, a scudding cloud drove over the face of the moon. Ned took advantage of it to shuffle back into cover on hands and knees. But he was too late. One of the men loosed off a shot and Ned felt as if he'd been slammed in the foot by a sledgehammer. But he kept on going and made ten yards further into the brush.

'Hey! Who's shooting at what?' came a slurred voice from the gang gathered outside the store.

'A wolf, I reckon,' shouted Dodds in reply.

He was answered by a general guffaw: 'Ain't no wolves round here, mister.'

'Well a bear, then, or a wild dog, or a mountain lion, how the hell should I know?'

There was more laughter from the drinkers who then lost interest.

'See anything?' asked Dodds.

'Nope. Might have been something. Mebbe it was nothing.'

'Go check it out,' said Dodds. 'We can't afford to take any chances.'

From his position upwind of the wagon, Daco, though he had got a lot nearer than Ned, had caught a lot less of what had been said. Time to go, in case Dodds and Lankton took it into their heads to beat through the bushes he was hiding in. Backing away, he circled the wagon, listened, stopped and listened again. All he heard was the rustle of the wind in the dry leaves. He took a few more steps and paused, then crept forward again. Above the wind he caught, away to his left, a low groan. Ahead of him he also heard a twig snap under a pair of boots stepping carefully through the grass. Then all went quiet again and a voice, which he recognized as Lankton's, called:

'Cain't see anything. I reckon it was some critter, like you said.'

Then the steps retreated and the night was left to the sighing wind and the moan.

Daco tracked it down.

Ned was sitting with his back against the trunk of a tree holding his foot. He looked up as he heard footsteps approach.

Daco held one finger to his lips for silence, pulled him to his feet and slung him across his shoulders. Then he headed back past Frenchie's store, keeping clear of the light, and started up the track. When they were well out of earshot of the wagon, he set Ned down by the side of the trail. Ned said he could hobble the rest of the way but needed an arm to hang on to. They made it back to camp without Ned passing out.

After administering a couple of large and not strictly medicinal doses of whiskey, Daco cleaned the wound and bandaged it up. It didn't look good.

Some bones were broken and would need resetting. It wasn't going to heal soon and he guessed Ned would be left with a permanent limp.

Even so, Ned perked up enough to tell about what he'd heard. When he finished, Daco said:

'What did they mean when they said they had to have spoil full of quartz and slate?'

'You get them where there's gold deposits. Find them together and you can start digging. All the claims round here have spoil heaps full of slate and quartz. The question is: what in tarnation do they want the stuff for? If it's spoil for ballast, any sort of rock would do. They don't need to haul themselves all the way up here, buy a wagon and team and load it up with left-overs from dead gold mines. Don't make sense. Then there was that other word, 'sillero' it sounded like.'

'Think it could have been Silveroo?'

'Maybe. Like I said, the wind was blowing the voices around.'

'It would fit with the yarn Dodds spun me. Silveroo's a place near Pocaloca, up in the Galejadas mountains . . . '

'Hold it there,' said Ned. 'I just remembered. They also talked about going to some place that sounded like 'galshaders'. I thought it was a river or maybe a town but it could have been what you just said.'

They chewed it over for a while but reached no conclusions. It made no sense. But something was going on. Men who robbed banks and were ready to kill didn't turn carters and hauliers just for fun. Daco thought a while. He needed to know more.

When Ned was asleep he buckled on his gunbelt and returned to the store. He settled behind a low earth wall which gave him good cover. From behind it he would see anything that travelled along the track which in one direction led down to the road to Chisholm and, in the other, up to the valley where most of the Burton Gulch claims were being worked.

He watched for an hour and then slept.

He was woken by the rumble of heavy cartwheels. The sky was just beginning to turn rosy and as he peered over the top of his wall he saw the two strangers driving Chuck Olson's cart up the track. A couple of saddle horses were hitched to the back of it. He let it pass and then followed, taking care not to be seen in growing light.

The cart toiled on for a half hour. From time to time Dodds stood up in the driver's seat and looked off the track every time they passed an abandoned claim. Once they stopped, he got down and inspected a heap of dirt and rocks that had been dug out by some hopeful, long-gone and doubtless long-dead miner. But it was clearly not what he was looking for, because each time he waved the cart on.

Now they were getting near the top of the gulch where the first strikes had been made. Here there were hardly any live claims, but none of the deserted workings they passed were what Dodds wanted. At last he found what he had come for. He lashed the wagon's brake fast, chocked the wheels, unhitched the saddle horses, which immediately started to graze, and let down the tailboard. Then he and Lankton started shovelling spoil.

Daco crawled through the low bushes and got as near as he dared. Neither of the two men spoke while they worked. But after a while they took a breather. They sat on a rock and rolled smokes. Daco had the drop on them. He could finish this now, with two bullets. But that was not his way. The decent man who uses the methods of the bad man stops being a decent man.

'I sure as hell hope all this is going to pay off,' said Lankton. 'I ain't worked as hard since I was in jail.'

'What was you in jail for?' said Dodds.

'Me and another feller robbed a train.'

'You got caught robbing a train?

What are you, careless or a loser?'

Lankton spat a jet of saliva at Dodds's feet.

'We got all that money from the bank and we eat like pigs,' he snarled. 'Just beans and bacon. I ain't had me a good piece of beefsteak meat in weeks.'

'Just wait till we get up to Pocaloca and you'll feed like a king. Ma makes the best pies in the county. Known for them. She wins prizes every Fourth of July. Tender, lean meat in gravy like the angels eat in paradise. So the quicker we fill the wagon, the sooner you'll get outside one of Mrs Dodds's Famous Meat Pies.'

Lankton scowled, threw down the rest of his cigarette, picked up his shovel and resumed loading the wagon.

Daco stayed where he was for another hour or so, but both men were too busy breaking their backs to talk. But he felt satisfied with what he'd learned. He now knew where the wagon was headed, which confirmed his suspicion that the answer to the mystery was up in the Galejadas mountains, around Silveroo and Pocaloca.

Just before noon, Dodds called a halt, raised and bolted the tailgate. He and Lankton didn't rest up but at once set off down the trail, with their saddle horses again hitched to the back of it. When they were out of sight, Daco emerged from his hideaway, stretched and walked back down to camp to see how Ned was doing.

9

Pocaloca

On his way back to camp, Daco stopped off at a claim that wasn't being worked but showed signs of life. Ned had told him he would find old Doc Fancy, the bone-setter, there. Doc Fancy, a once respectable medical man who'd been struck off for being fond of the bottle, wasn't much of a hand with a pick and shovel but he was the best man around to fix Ned's leg. He reckoned the foot was in a bad way. He accepted a drink. Then he added that it was a foot that might mend straight if mended right. He held out the tin cup which travelled with him wherever he went, took another deep pull, and set about his work with surprising precision.

Daco laid in supplies from the stores

and arranged with Chuck Olson to keep Ned victualled until he and Mack got back. Then he had a bite to eat, saddled his horse, said goodbye to Ned, rode down the mountain and joined the Chisholm road. It was a sight hotter down on the plain than up in Burton Gulch and he didn't force his horse. By the time he hit town, the western sky was a wide blush of crimson fire.

He found Mack at the Lucky Penny saloon, having his dinner.

'I been eating here. It ain't bad. Anyways, I thought I'd steer clear of Ma Kennedy's till I was strong enough to take it. I been through one ordeal. I don't want to face another,' he said with a rueful grin. 'That woman sure has a heavy hand with a stewpot.'

He was more or less as good as new. He'd need to keep his arm strapped for a couple of days yet, for the support, but he didn't need the sling. He'd ridden a half-dozen miles that morning, and galloped one of them, without feeling any bad effects.

While Mack worked at his teeth with a toothpick, Daco ordered a plate of the same chow as Mack had just finished. As he ate, he filled Mack in with his news, about how Ned had got a slug in the foot but was on the mend and how Dodds and Lankton had picked up a load of spoil and were hauling it up to Pocaloca, though why he hadn't been able to work out.

Mack thought a moment. Then he said:

'Listen, Daco. Pocaloca is silver country. I told you about that old timer who went up there prospecting for gold and found silver instead, only there wasn't much of it, only just enough for him to call the place Silveroo. I guess it was his little joke. Now let's say some Johnny-come-lately arrives in Clayton with samples showing he's struck gold in Silveroo. Reckons there's nuggets lying around waiting to be picked up by anyone who cares to bend down, and ore that pays two grains a ton. Is your mouth watering?'

'Sure is,' said <u>Ned</u>.

'Would you buy a claim like that if it was for sale?'

'The price would be too steep for me. But I reckon I could get a syndicate. You, for a start, Chuck Olson and some of the other fellers might throw in if the deal was right.'

'You'd want proof the place was a payer?'

'Sure would. I'd look for the signs.'

'There's signs and signs. Old Chuck Olson's like me, he ain't one of them who think a man can't say where gold is unless he can see it with his naked eye. Book-learned men like him and me don't need to see *colour*. We want to see the sedimentary cosying up to the igneous. If I saw sedimentary and igneous lying down together I'd sink a shaft without waiting to see colour.'

'You're losing me.'

'What I'm saying is most men looking for gold would believe a claim was worth buying if they were shown a handful of nuggets and a spoil heap with quartz, slate, granodiorite and similar in it. Am I right?'

'I guess so.'

'I reckon what Dodds is up to is salting his mine up at Silveroo so he can sell it, knowing that it's worthless. When he's got his price, you won't see him for dust.'

Daco lit a smoke and sat a while without speaking. Then he said:

'What you say fits the facts right enough. But I can't see it's the crime of the century. There's lots of men would like to part you from your money and don't care much how they do it.'

'It ain't right but, like you say, there's lot worse goes on than salting a claim. Ain't that much money in it neither given all the time and bother it takes to set up. But one thing I do know, which is this. Dodds and Lankton are shooting at most everybody I know, including me. They're not shooting straight just now, thanks be, but that could change. But if they're prepared to kill — '

161

'And rob banks,' Ned chipped in.

' . . . then there's more to all this than meets the eye.'

'Sure am sorry your partner got it in the foot,' said Daco. 'First time I set eyes on Lankton I knew he was a wrong 'un. But I had friend Dodds pegged for a regular, straight-up sort of feller. But wherever he goes there's mayhem. I got a score to settle with him and I can't wait no longer. If you ain't ready to come with me, then I go by myself. When I settle Dodds's hash I'll see you get back what he stole from you at the bank.'

'Stow that talk, Daco. It's my quarrel too. He got away with a large chunk of what me and Ned worked hard for. I've got some evening-up to do on my own account. You ain't going to cut me out of this.'

They shook hands on it, and then Mack said:

'Now I got a piece of news for you. Yesterday, I was sitting on the porch here watching the world go by when I see a familiar face. Feller name of Clip Dougan . . .

'Works as nightman in Casey's rooming joint in Clayton,' said Daco. 'I know him.'

'He and me go way back. I bought him a drink and then he suddenly comes out with something that brought me up short. Now, Clip's got a son who's Clayton's assay officer. According to Clip's boy, nobody's registered a claim of any sort with him up anywhere near Pocaloca in the last couple of months. I then checked with the assay officer here in Chisholm and he said the same. No claims registered anywhere in the Galejadas. So here's an odd thing. If Dodds wants to spread the word he's got a strike he's willing to part with for cash, why hasn't he made sure he's got a piece of paper showing his legal entitlement to sell what he says he owns?'

Daco scratched his head: 'Maybe the kind of taker he's got in mind don't go a bundle on legal papers. Could be lots of reasons. Still, it jars with what you'd expect. But that don't affect what we do next.'

'Sure don't,' said Mack. 'We go to Pocaloca.'

'Agreed. No need to go looking for Dodds and Lankton, because we know that's where they're headed.'

'And we also know why they're going there: to salt a mine, make it look a tempting proposition. That's where I come in. We'll have to get close to them. They don't know me from a horse's ass, so I could be their first customer to come along and swallow the bait.'

'You sure they won't remember you from the bank?'

'They had a lot to think about and studying faces wasn't one of them. No, it was all over too fast.'

'Maybe, but we'll think about it. I don't want you taking unnecessary risks. Meanwhile, where does the Dodds family fit into all this?'

'If there is one,' said Mack. 'Like I said, I never heard tell of them when

I was trying my luck in the Galejadas.'

'But what if there really is a pie-lady called Mrs Dodds?' asked Daco. 'And what about this sister, Annie?'

'We'll think about that when we get there. But not now,' said Mack, getting to his feet. 'I don't suppose you got much sleep last night and I'm ready to hit the hay. Good night, Daco. See you in the morning.'

Daco stayed a while where he was. He ordered a beer and thought about the web he'd got caught up in. Then he went to bed too.

Next day, after they'd got outside a good breakfast, they walked down to the general stores to pick up supplies. They replenished their ammunition and bought bacon, beans, flour, coffee. At Mack's insistence — 'got to look the part' — they also got in a stock of mining equipment: picks, shovels, prospector's hammers, a couple of cradles, washing pans. At the Lucky Penny's stables they went looking for a pony or a buckskin cayuse to haul the goods they'd bought. In the end, they bought a slab-sided mule for fifteen dollars.

They took the direct route to Pocaloca, heading out straight west. They made fair time and rejoined the Clayton cut-off by late morning the next day. There they rested up till evening. Before they set off again, Daco climbed atop a tall rock to spy out the lie of the land. Maybe three miles ahead he saw buzzards circling in the sky. When they got near the place, they tied the horses to thick stems of sage-brush and investigated. Only case-hardened army horses don't mind dead bodies, and Daco tethered them real fast. He had no intention of being lost in the desert a second time.

Daco recognized Crants, or what was left of him, by his boots which he had twice seen close up.

'He didn't die peaceful,' said Mack, leaning over the corpse and pointing to the skull. 'He was shot in the head.'

Crants had been buried in a shallow grave in the sand. But some large animal had pulled him clear and started a meal which had been continued by the buzzards. It would be the worms' turn next. They dug a deeper hole, placed Crants's remains in it, shovelled sand over them and raised a cairn of rocks to protect them against further attacks. Then they went their way.

By noon the next day the trail had begun to climb and as it got higher the vegetation became more abundant. It was bigger, lusher, greener. Stunted sage and mesquite were replaced by bushes and trees. Ahead, the foothills of the Galejadas rose a couple of thousand feet above them. They could see the first sugar pines and silver spruce. It was not so hot now and they could again travel by day and rest by night.

They saw nothing of Dodds and Lankton. It had rained here more than once and the trail bore no trace of cartwheels. But they hadn't expected to come across their tracks. With a loaded wagon, they'd make slow progress and would be well back to their rear. Daco and Mack could count on a good few days for getting to know the lie of the land before they showed up anywhere near Silveroo.

It took another day and a half to get to Pocaloca, not a town exactly, more a settlement which still had a temporary look about it, as if the people had not yet decided to stay. It sat in a dip in a plateau of rolling prairie land. Above reared the Galejadas whose peaks stayed white all year round.

Daco recalled Clip saying how thirty years ago it was not even a one-horse sort of town. It had grown some since those times, but it wasn't the sort of place you'd buy a ticket to go to. There was a store, a church and a blacksmith, and maybe a score of timber houses, but nothing like a hotel or rooming-house. But there was a bar in the stores, where they got a drink.

'Passing through?' said a man they took to be the Jacob Galt who proclaimed over the front door to be the proprietor.

'Nope. Aiming to bide a while. But there ain't no hotel to stay at.'

'Mrs Doherty lets rooms to gents she considers suitable.'

Mrs Doherty, a firm but kindly widow of around sixty years of age, liked the look of them and they agreed terms. After they'd unloaded their equipment into a lean-to and settled the mule in the stables, there was still enough left of the day for a short foray.

As they rode they saw a few homesteads and large numbers of sheep grazing the flat grasslands. A mile from the faint trail that they were following they saw a solitary man mending a fence, but no one else.

Over dinner, while Mrs Doherty was piling their plates high, Daco said: 'I don't suppose you get many strangers venturing up this far?'

'Not as a rule. Buyers for the sheep in season, men selling new kinds of sheep-dip and feeds and the like. But no crowds. Still, these last weeks I've had quite a few gentlemen staying under my roof. Said they were from the railroad company. They went out early and came back late. I couldn't figure out what they did with themselves. More pie?'

After they'd eaten they strolled across the way to drink a glass of Jake Galt's whiskey. Evidently, Mrs Doherty's railmen boarders had done the same on a regular basis, for Jake was expecting them. He was bursting with information which he spilled eagerly, as men do when they are loose-tongued by nature and denied an audience by circumstances.

What he was burning to tell was the complicated tale of a boundary dispute he was having with a neighbour who was trying to get his hands on a good stretch of riverbank that didn't belong to him, no way . . .

Daco and Mack nodded and said: 'Man's got some nerve' and the like. Then he got on to the folks that lived in Pocaloca itself.

'Hundred and fifty-two souls,' he

said, proudly. 'Knowed 'em all since before I was put in long pants. Except for Mrs Dodds and Annie. They came later, I reckon about three years since. Before they come here, though, they had a place up yonder, at Silveroo, maybe an hour's ride up in the hills.'

'What happened to Mr Dodds?' asked Mack.

'Sad case. He was a book-learned man who came up here to try his hand at sheep-rearing. He'd just about got himself set up when he was killed. Accident. He and Annie, his little girl, were out riding. Story goes his horse stepped into a patch of soft sand or fresh-turned ground up to its fetlock. Threw Mr Dodds. Broke his back. Annie galloped off for help but her horse was too varminty for her, it fell and rolled on her. He died and she lived. But she's never walked straight since that day. Nice girl, always a smile. Must be all of eighteen now. When Mr Dodds was gone, Mrs Dodds sold the stock and settled here. Plays the harmonium in church every Sunday. Never misses. Everybody likes them.'

'Didn't they have any sons could have looked out for the sheep and carry on what their pa had started?' Mack asked innocently.

'There was one boy. Billy. He was four or five years older than Annie. But he was nothing like the rest of the family. Of course, everybody liked Billy Dodds; he could charm the birds out of the trees. But he was trouble from the start. He'd steal the shirt off your back. His folks couldn't correct him, nobody could. He'd left home by the time his pa was killed. He comes back now and then, when he's broke or in hot water. But I ain't seen him in a good while.'

Afterwards Mack said, as they strolled back to Mrs Doherty's: 'No wonder I never heard of Dodds and his family. I passed through here a good ten years since. They hadn't arrived then.'

They paused for a moment outside a single-storey house which Jacob Galt had told them was the Dodds's place. A woman wearing a long-skirted, grey bombazine dress and a plain mob cap was hoeing between the rows of her vegetable garden. She looked up and stared. Then she looked embarrassed.

'Sorry for staring. Seeing you stopped there, I thought you might be bringing news of Billy. Billy Dodds is my son.'

News I have but not the sort you'd want to hear, thought Daco.

'We don't get many strangers in Pocaloca so we're always short of news,' she went on. 'Why don't you come in, anyway? I got some biscuits I baked this morning.'

They stayed half an hour, gave such news as they had, and listened while Mrs Dodds told them how the family had come to Pocaloca and about the tragedy which had struck her husband and left her daughter — who was as sweet-natured as Jake Galt had said — with a withered leg. As they left, Mrs Dodds said that since they were intending to stay in town a while they were to be sure and call again.

'Well that's cleared up something that's been bothering me,' said Daco.

'What's that?'

'When the old timer who christened the place Silveroo filed his claim all them years ago, the land didn't belong to anybody. You can't file claims on land that already belongs to somebody. But when Dodds's father brought his family up here, he either brought it through the federal government land sale to raise sheep on or else he bought it from someone who had done so before him. No wonder Dodds never registered a claim. He didn't have to. That land belongs to the family.'

'And what difference does that make?' asked Mack.

'I ain't sure. But I'll work on it.'

But he hadn't made any more sense of it the next day when they rode up to Silveroo to scout around.

Silveroo was a flat plain, half a mile wide and a mile long, which sat between two towering flanks of the Galejadas. It was split by a river that flowed west and was fed by streams from small canyons that fissured the slopes of mountains on each side. They followed the river to the western end. There the land dropped away as gently as on the Pocaloca side. Because it ran east to west, it got good sun. But it was poor pasture, only capable of supporting a couple of sheep per acre.

On the northern side, in the lee of a bulge in the side of the mountain, was a cabin made of caulked logs. This had to be the old Dodds place, the one they'd called Silveroo. A garden had been staked out with a picket fence and there was a barn for animals. It had seen better days. The roofs of both buildings had mostly withstood winter snows but the fences had been brought down.

They came across a few animal tracks, deer or maybe elk, and birds of prey called over their heads. Otherwise there was no sign of life, no sign that men had dug the earth in pursuit of precious metals. Silveroo was deserted.

10

In the High Galejadas

Tucker Lankton got down off the wagon and led the horses over the narrow bridge. They'd been on the trail from Burton Gulch long enough for his patience to have worn paper thin. His fancy boots were scuffed and worn down and his sharp clothes were torn. He hadn't shaved for days. These were things that mattered to a man whose appearance was a part of his stock-in-trade as a professional card-player.

But at least it was cooler at this altitude and the horses, with green grass to graze on now, had regained the strength they had used up crossing the desert.

'How much further we got to go?'

Dodds in the driving seat clicked his tongue to encourage the horses and pointed to a ridge 500 feet above them.

'Silveroo Pass,' he said. 'Once we get there, maybe a couple of hours up this trail, we'll have flat country and steady going all the way to Silveroo. We'll be there before nightfall.'

Lankton grunted and went on leading the horses.

Three hours later, a little later than Dodds's estimate, they breasted the rim. Here they came out again into the sun which threw long shadows across the long plain that stretched out between the flanks of thc Galejadas. Dodds set a course for the north side where, in time, Lankton made out a tumble-down cabin.

'No place like home. I was a kid here,' said Dodds by way of explanation and he grinned as he jumped down from the cart.

While Lankton unhitched the team, hobbled them and the saddle horses and left them to graze, Dodds collected wood and lit a fire for a meal. Both men were too tired to do any more that night than to collapse into a couple of makeshift beds.

Next morning, they saddled up the horses, strapped on a pick, shovels and a small barrel containing some of the gunpowder they had retrieved along the way.

Dodds led the way east until they came to a fast-running stream which had carved a deep groove in the mountainside. Here it had once been dammed with an earthwork which had been mostly washed away by winter rains. On the banks of the stream were mounds, partly covered with grass.

'Silveroo,' he said, 'soon to be Golderoo!'

They dismounted and staked the horses far enough downstream for the blasting not to scare them. Then Dodds took the pick and climbed thirty feet up the valley, stopping at a point where the sides narrowed. He swung the pick and had soon gouged out a shallow impression maybe four feet across.

While he rested, Lankton carted the

earth and rock away and began making a dump of it. They repeated the operation until they had a hole a man could walk six feet into.

'We've hit rock,' called Dodds. 'Get the explosive.'

And so the day proceeded. Dodds swung the pick while Lankton shovelled. Sometimes, for variety, they swapped tools. From time to time, the noise of an explosion split the lonely silence. When the noise died away and the fumes had dispersed, they resumed work. They stopped to rest and eat but by the time they began to lose the light, they'd burrowed around fifteen feet into the side of the mountain.

'Tomorrow,' said Dodds, 'we'll cut some timber. This is going to need shoring up. But that's it for now.'

They kept up this rhythm for another two days.

Then they fetched Chuck Olson's wagon.

* * *

Daco and Mack rode every which way around Silveroo, looking for the old silver workings. They found nothing to show that humans had had any dealings thereabouts for years. Every day they expected to see some sign that Dodds and Lankton had arrived at the cabin with Chuck Olson's wagon. But every day they found Silveroo undisturbed.

One night, at supper, Mrs Doherty said:

'There ain't nothing for you boys at Silveroo. It got all worked out.'

'No harm in looking,' said Mack. 'The man who never made an effort never made anything.'

Later, over a glass of Galt's whiskey, Daco said:

'We're getting nowhere. Maybe we should pay Mrs Dodds another call. Be only polite, seeing Silveroo belongs to the family, to get her say-so to us wandering round her property.'

Next morning they went calling.

'Mind?' said Mrs Dodds. 'Of course I don't mind. The land's not doing anybody any good the way things are, so you might as well see what you can find. Poke around all you want. But I warn you. Lots have looked and never came up with anything.'

'If we do strike lucky, you can be sure you'll be the first to hear and the first to benefit.'

'That's nice to know. But I shan't be ordering new curtains just yet,' she added with a twinkle in her eye.

As they had done for six or seven mornings in a row, they strapped a pick and shovel to Blackie, the stronger of the two horses, and dropped hammers and chisels in the saddlebag. Then they rode up to Silveroo to start another search. When they got there, Daco reined in his horse and thought.

'Maybe we missed something,' he said. 'Maybe we should go back to the beginning. Let's start again with the cabin.'

They hadn't seen the place for several days, but when they saw it again they sensed it was different. There was nothing much to see — no smoke at the chimney and Chuck Olson's wagon wasn't there — but the property had been tidied up. There were no signs of life. Then came the distant sound of an explosion.

'Gunpowder,' said Mack. 'Could you tell where it came from?'

They rode east, skirting the bottom of the mountain, keeping a close watch for anything that moved.

If it hadn't been for the wagon, they'd have ridden past the spot. Now empty, it stood on the bank of a stream which ran down a narrow valley and joined the main watercourse, which flowed to the west.

They tethered the horses in a stand of stunted trees where they would not be seen and approached with caution, stopping to look and listen and not going on until they were sure it was safe. To the right of the wagon, a little way up the valley, were the workings: an open shaft and a heap of fresh spoil. The place was deserted.

Mack had a look first at the spoil.

'Most of this is new-dug soil and rock. No one would believe there's gold anywhere nearabouts. But in with it is mixed pockets of the quartz and slate and the rest of the stuff they hauled all the way up here from Burton Gulch. There's enough of it here to paint a rosy picture. They've made a good job of it. If they show this and wave a few nuggets under a hundred gold-sniffing noses, I reckon ninety-nine gold-hungry prospectors would fall for it.'

Then he crouched and entered the tunnel which was now shored up with timber props and ran into the mountain far enough for a man to need a lantern to see by.

Daco did not go with him. He sat on his heels, tipped his hat to the back of his head and pondered their discovery.

Salting the mine needed an effort out of proportion to the return. No one was going to pay big money for an untested claim which might be a winner or peter out within two days. So was there another angle? An idea snagged his mind, just out of reach. It made him uncomfortable. What was Dodds really up to?

His thoughts were put to flight by the sound of approaching horses. He didn't even have time to shout a warning into the tunnel. Then he climbed further up the valley, found a vantage point and a rock from which he could see without being seen. He had just settled in when Dodds and Lankton appeared. They dismounted, tethered their horses to the wagon and, still talking, made for the workings. They were still twenty yards short of it when Mack came out of the tunnel, blinking as he emerged into the bright sunshine. When Dodds and Lankton saw him, they stopped in their tracks. The next moment each man had a gun in his fist.

'Just hold it there, stranger,' said Dodds. 'This here is private property and you're trespassing.'

'Put your gun up, son,' said Mack. 'I'm in the same business as you.'

'You a prospector?' asked Dodds.

'I came up here as a speculation, you might say. Had a feeling about the place. But you beat me to it. Looks like you struck gold here.'

'How can you tell?' snapped Lankton.

'When an Indian is following a trail, he looks out for signs. I done the same.'

'What signs?' said Lankton.

'The kind of earth and rocks you fellers been digging out. The signs all say gold.'

Dodds cast a sideways glance at Lankton, a look of triumph which he understood, for it said: *The plan worked!*

'Check him out,' he ordered Lankton. 'Get his gun.'

'I ain't carrying no gun,' said Mack. 'But I got me a rifle. It's on my horse — '

'Where's your horse?'

'Horses,' Mack corrected. 'I ride one and the other carries my gear. Got them tethered under those trees yonder.'

'Show me,' said Dodds, and with his gun he motioned Mack to lead the way.

As they walked Mack continued talking as if he weren't in deep trouble, as if he didn't know that one word out of place, one false move, and he was dead meat.

Daco, gun drawn, moving as quietly as a mountain cat, followed and found cover in a dip of the land.

' . . . only I been looking for silver. It's what a man would expect to find in a place called Silveroo. So maybe my feeling wasn't what I thought it was about. I was looking for the wrong thing.'

Dodds gave both horses the once over. The tools confirmed what the stranger had said.

'You got two saddles and no bedroll. How come?'

'The sorrel was walking a mite lame yesterday, so I saddled up the big black too, in case I needed to switch. As for the bedroll, I ain't living out just yet. I will when I strike something worth exploring. Until then I got a room in Pocaloca, renting it from Mrs Doherty. You know her?'

'And your name?'

'Jed Donohue.'

'All right, Donohue. As far as I can tell you're on the level. Can't be too careful with a gold strike. But you ain't wanted around here. So why don't you just get on your horse and ride away.'

'Sure am sorry to hear you say that. There's always a lot of heavy work with a claim. I was just wondering if you couldn't do with an extra hand. Some of that shoring up work don't look too safe.'

'This ain't no place for you,' said Lankton. 'You heard the man.'

'Then maybe you'd consider a straight business proposition. I'll buy the claim. Cash.'

'It ain't for sale. So sling your hook, mister,' snarled Lankton, and he produced his gun and put the barrel against Mack's head.

'Hold it, partner,' said Dodds. 'No

need to be hasty. It's true the claim ain't for sale. But that's no reason for not hearing what the man's got to say.'

Lankton lowered his gun.

Daco's finger, which had started to squeeze the trigger of the gun which was pointing straight at Lankton's heart, relaxed.

'What sort of money,' Dodds went on, 'are you ready to put where your mouth is?'

'Now that depends on a lot of things. I like a claim to show colour. You got colour to show me? Next, you'll have a paper from the assay office saying how much the ore will pay per ton. You got those papers?'

'I can show you colour right now,' said Dodds. From his pocket he produced two or three small pellets of brassy metal and passed them to Mack who examined them closely.

'Looks like gold in the free state, sure enough,' he said, returning them to their owner. 'That's good, provided you got them from around here. Now what about them papers?'

'The assay showed it'll pay a couple of grains a ton.'

'That's good too. But you'll appreciate I can't just take your say-so. I got to see for myself.'

Dodds squeezed out a friendly smile, the one he used when he was working on a soft touch.

'Sure you can see them papers,' he said. 'They're back at the house. All signed and certified by the assay officer of Clayton Creek.'

'What are we waiting for. Let's go,' said Mack.

Daco, shaking his head admiringly at his partner's cool nerve, watched him hitch Blackie to his own mount and ride behind the wagon which Lankton was driving. He didn't hurry and Daco followed on foot at a safe distance, loping along without working up a sweat and wondering how Mack would handle the situation when they reached the cabin. So far, he'd done pretty good.

Over the noise of hoofs and wagon wheels, Lankton said in a low voice so that 'Donohue' wouldn't hear:

'The guy's not on the level. It don't sound right. I'm sure I saw him before, but I can't place him. Why didn't you let me put a bullet in his head?'

'Because he knows his business is why. You learn from a man like that. We let him look at the assay report, he says why isn't there more such and such, or why is the so and so missing, and the like. They're the questions that'll be asked when sale time comes for real and I ain't sure I got all the answers. So Donohue will be a trial run. I aim to get some useful tips that will make my pitch more convincing.'

'And when you've milked him for all you can get out of him, then we kill him?'

'Maybe not. If he makes us an offer, we'll agree to sell and let him go get the money. When he comes back with it, then we kill him.'

'No sale, but we keep the cash,'

sniggered Lankton. 'Get paid twice! I'll drink to that!'

'And if word gets out when he's gone down the mountain that he's bought a gold mine at Silveroo, those railroad boys will be half sold on the idea that it's a genuine, authentic strike. The deal will be as good as signed before they even get here.'

Lankton was so tickled with the idea he guffawed and slapped Dodds on the back.

When they reached the cabin Mack looked around him, caught a glimpse of Daco diving into cover out of the corner of his eye, and said pleasantly:

'Nice place you got here. With a bit of work, this would make a good base for me. Now what about them reports?'

Dodds led the way into a room furnished with four straight backed chairs, a table and not much else. He removed a loose floorboard over which a worm-eaten rug had been thrown and produced a satchel. From it, he took a bundle of papers.

Mack took the papers, pulled up a chair and spread the papers on the table. He read in silence. After a while, he said:

'Where's your title to the claim? You did register it?'

'Think I'm a mutt? 'Course I did,' said Dodds. 'But the man at the office said he had to confirm with the state office in Templeton before he could issue the deed. Said it would take time. A formality, but I'd have to wait. Meantime, he gave me this. It's a receipt.'

He handed over a paper with the stamp of Clayton assay office certifying that a claim was being finalized. Mack, who'd had many dealings with Clip's boy, Brett Dougan, didn't recognize the signature. Anyway, old Clip had said Brett hadn't registered any claims for two months. The paper was a forgery. But he smiled and said:

'Fair enough. I guess that's all in order. Now let's talk turkey, by which I mean money. Way I see it, the claim looks good on paper, but there's no guarantee that there's much life in it. I got no way of knowing if it might give up on me tomorrow, like the silver did in the old days. That makes it a risky investment.'

He stopped, furrowed his brow and considered.

'You can't talk my property down like that,' said Dodds. 'A man can never tell how much money exactly he'll dig out of a mountain. But the signs are good, and you said you were a man who went by the signs.'

'If your claim is such a good prospect,' said Mack, 'how come you and your partner are so ready to sell?'

'We ain't, like I told you. But if the price is right, we could be persuaded. Ain't that right, Tucker?'

Lankton added a surly note: 'Sure is, because speaking for myself, I ain't keen on breaking my back digging holes in the ground. I'm no mountain boy. A town is where I like to be best. I like to feel a sidewalk under my feet when it rains.'

'Look,' said Mack gravely, 'this is what I'm prepared to lay on the table. For full ownership of the claim we're talking about, I'm prepared to offer you,' he hesitated, 'two thousand dollars.'

Dodds laughed, then said 'Six.'

Mack stood up as if he were about to leave, then raised his offer. Dodds laughed again and lowered his.

Outside, crouching under a broken window, Daco heard the bartering close at $3,000.

'You drive a hard bargain, Mr . . . ?' asked Mack.

'Dodds.'

' . . . Mr Dodds. Now let's shake on it. Maybe you got a bottle at hand so we can seal our business and put it to bed. Then I'll be on my way. It'll take two days. Half cash, half gold be all right for you?'

'That suits me fine. But when you go, leave the black stallion here. You'll get it back when you come with the money. Call it insurance, a returnable deposit.'

Mack hesitated a moment, then

nodded and turned to leave. Just as Daco thought he'd talked his way clear out of trouble, Lankton cried:

'I remember where I seen him before! He was in the bank the day we raided it.'

'Shut your mouth, you fool!' cried Dodds, for he saw $3000 being blown away by the words. Even if Lankton was right and this 'Donohue' had been in the bank, there had been nothing to link them to the robbery. But now that Lankton had opened his fool mouth, Donohue was in a position to identify them.

He could not be allowed to live.

Daco too realized that Lankton had signed Mack's death warrant.

Without waiting a moment longer, he burst in through the window, with a six-shooter in his fist.

11

The Reckoning

'Hands in the air and keep them there,' said Daco. 'Mack, get their shooters.'

Lankton's jaw dropped in surprise when he recognized the man who'd jumped through the window and now held a gun on them. But Dodds recovered more quickly. As Mack emptied Lankton's holster, he spun round real fast, putting Mack between him and Daco. Then he turned and was through the door before Daco could get off a clear shot at him.

Mack was taken off his guard. Taking advantage of the surprise, Lankton took a wild swing and caught him hard enough to land him on the seat of his pants. As Mack went down, he dropped Lankton's gun. Lankton bent down to pick it up, but Daco's Colt barked and the gun was sent skittering across the floor out of his reach.

'Don't move or the next one's for you,' he barked.

Silence surged back into the space emptied by the blast of the shot. Through it came the sound of hoof-beats.

'Looks like your partner's gone and left you high and dry, Tucker,' said Daco. 'Like they say, there's no honour among thieves. Mack, get his gun again and this time hang on to it. Keep him covered.'

Mack sat up, rubbing his belly. He retrieved Lankton's gun and pointed it at its owner.

'I'm going to scout round outside and check if Dodds is really gone. We heard a horse, but that don't necessarily mean it had a rider on its back.'

The cabin door was open. Daco peered cautiously round it. There wasn't a lot of cover, but there were plenty of places to hide behind the low walls, in the barn and among bushes tall and thick enough to conceal a dozen men. And Dodds, who'd been part raised in the place, knew every corner of it and would make the most of his knowledge.

Chuck's wagon had not moved. The team and the saddle horses — his, Mack's and Lankton's — stood patiently grazing. After a few moments Daco saw a movement in a patch of brush. Then a bird flew up out of it and resumed feeding. Daco relaxed. Dodds had gone, at least for the time being, but not for ever.

Dodds had a lot riding on what he'd come this far to do and he wasn't going to stop now. But there wasn't much sense going after him. He knew the hills round about like the back of his hand and could be anywhere. Best sit tight and wait. He'd be back.

Daco returned to the cabin. There he found Lankton holding his gun to Mack's head.

'Your partner here is getting slow,' said Lankton, whose eyes were shining with anger, or maybe something else. 'That's twice I outsmarted him. Easy as taking toffee from a baby. Now it's your turn to throw your gun down, so do it.'

'Sorry, Daco, must be getting old,' said Mack. 'He jumped me.'

Daco did as he was told. When a man with a gun who has a crazy look in his eye tells you to do something, you do it.

'My partner may be getting slow, Tucker, but at least he's still here. Not like yours. He's gone. Left you to rescue yourself.'

'Sure, and I done it too. I rescued myself without anybody's help.'

'So what's the next move to be, Tucker? It's your call. You're the one with the gun.'

'I'm getting out. I want a horse and this is how we're going to do it.'

Obeying Lankton's orders, Daco backed out of the door and across the patch in front of the cabin. Lankton, still with his gun at Mack's head, followed and stopped when they reached the horses. Then he reversed the gun in his hand

and, holding the barrel, slugged Mack from behind. Mack went down. Then he swung up into the saddle of the nearest horse, Daco's black stallion.

'Running out, Tucker?' said Daco.

'I'm going to find Dodds. We got unfinished business. He's gone to ground and I know where he'll be.'

'The moment you're out of sight, we go down the mountain and fetch the law. You robbed a bank and we can testify it was you and Dodds done it.'

Just as Lankton was thinking what to do about this, Daco pursed his lips and whistled. Blackie suddenly bucked and reared up on his hind legs, tipping his rider out of the saddle. Lankton sprawled in the dust, momentarily winded. Then Daco was on him, straddling him, crashing a right and a left into his face. He turned his man on his stomach, pulled his arms behind him and bound them fast with Lankton's own neckerchief.

He whistled again and Blackie trotted up obediently. From his saddlebag,

Daco took a length of rawhide which he used to tie Lankton's feet. Only when his man was immobilized did he attend to Mack.

Mack groaned and started coming round. Daco sat him up, wiped the blood from his head and then helped him back into the cabin. Out in the open he felt exposed. Dodds was out there, maybe nearer than was comfortable. Then he returned for Lankton who by this time was spitting venom.

'Stow it,' said Daco, when they were inside. 'You got sapped twice too and you ain't got Mack's excuse of being real old.'

'Here, who are you calling old?' said Mack, raising an indignant grin.

'Way I see it, Tucker, you ain't got many choices,' said Daco. 'That bank job will take care of your future, which will be thirty years behind bars. Unless, that is, you co-operate. You co-operate and we'll put in a good word, make it so they go easier on you.'

'You could start by telling us where

you stashed the money you and Dodds stole,' said Mack. 'Some of it was mine and I want it back. We know you spent a chunk of it buying Chuck Olson's wagon. What you do with the rest of it?'

Lankton glared at them but said nothing.

'You just think about it,' said Daco, 'while I take a look at these papers. Mack, keep an eye out for Dodds. We don't want any nasty surprises.'

Mack moved to the window and peered out.

Daco leaned over the papers, which were still spread out on the table, but though he looked at them hard they added nothing to what he already knew, which was that Dodds had Clayton's assay office certificates saying his samples tested positive for gold, that the samples had in reality come from Burton Gulch, and that no claim had been registered because the land already belonged to Dodds, or at least to the family.

'Make anything of them?' called

Mack from his post at the window.

'It don't make sense. Unless . . . '

Suddenly Daco became excited.

'Mack, remember Mrs Doherty saying she'd had railroad men boarding in her house? Now what do you suppose they were doing up here?'

'What railroad engineers up country always do. Scouting for routes, I guess.'

'You ever hear tell of any plans to run a railroad through the Galejadas?'

'Sure. A few years back people in Clayton got very excited over talk about the railroad branching off south-west to make a direct link between Missouri and the states west of the Galejadas. But it never came to anything.'

'Well that's our answer. They're planning to bring the railroad through here!'

'Makes sense. Silveroo is the lowest pass in the Galejadas.'

'Think about it, Mack. The railroad company needs this piece of land. As things stand, it ain't worth much. It's too high to farm and as pasture it's poor. But if it turned out there's gold on it, it would become very valuable and the price could go sky high!'

'So that's why Dodds salted the mine! It was to jack up the price he'd get for the land! He never intended to sell the mine as a going concern. So when I offered to buy it, he was happy to let me ride back to town to fetch the purchase money. If word got out there was a strike up here, and you can't keep news like that quiet for long, the railroad company would get to hear about it and be softened up before the bidding even started. Those rail fellers ain't prospectors, they wouldn't know the difference.'

Then he thought for a moment:

'And when I got back with the money, he'd have taken it and blown a hole in my head. This Dodds sure is an evil son of a hog.'

'No need to take it personal, Mack. That's how he treats everybody when they've outlived their usefulness. He ran out on me in Clayton. Then when we were in the desert he left me to the tender mercies of Tucker here. It was Dodds who shot Crants, wasn't it, Tucker? And you're next in line.'

Lankton bit his lip, then said defiantly: 'Nuts to that. Him and me, we got a deal.'

'Sure. You break your back helping him to salt the mine and in return you get a big share of the land sale money. You're wrong. A bullet in the head is all you'll get.'

Suddenly Mack said: 'Daco, come and take a look. There's something going on.'

Daco peered carefully through the window. Smoke was rising from the roofless barn fifty yards away. A small fire had been lit inside. From it what looked like a small meteor flew towards the cabin. It landed a yard or two short of the front door.

'It's Dodds. He's shooting fire arrows,' said Mack. 'He's going to burn us out.'

Lankton, pale-faced and with a

tremble in his voice, said: 'That's not it. I know what he's going to do. We brought a big keg of gunpowder up here for blowing rock for a tunnel on the claim. We took half of it to the mine. The rest is in the room back of us. He's going to blow the cabin up and us with it!'

'Go and check, Mack.'

Lankton had begun to sweat. Daco could smell his fear.

There was a thud as a second arrow landed on a part of the roof that had survived the years.

'Yep,' said Mack as he returned. 'There's a half-barrel back there. He's finding his range, Daco. Only a matter of time before the whole place goes up. This place is as dry as tinder.'

'We'd best get out while we can. We can't take Lankton. Pity about that. He'd slow us down too much, so we'll have to leave him. Still, a quick death is better than thirty years in jail.'

Lankton begged and pleaded not to be left behind.

'Tell us where you keep the money you stole from the bank,' said Daco, 'and I'll give it some thought.'

'I'll tell you,' Lankton cried. 'We divided it. My share is behind a loose brick in the chimney. I don't know where Dodds put his.'

Following Lankton's instructions, Daco retrieved the money which was wrapped in newspaper.

'Now what have we here,' he said.

He opened the packet, then whistled in surprise and grinned. 'A lot more than the six hundred they took off you, Mack. But we'll count it later and return it when we get out of this fix. Just bag it up with them legal papers in the satchel.'

By now three more arrows had landed, two of them direct hits on the back room which was largely open to the skies. A fire had started up in the wind-dried plank floor.

'Is there a back way out of this place?' he asked Lankton. He cut the rawhide around his legs but left his wrists tied. He wanted him able to move around but not able to use his hands.

Lankton nodded.

From his post at the front of the house, Mack said the arrows had stopped coming. There was no need for them now, for the house was a raging inferno. So there was no way of telling if Dodds was still in the barn.

'Here, Mack, take my gun and fire a few rounds at him. Give him something to think about. Then we get out of here.'

By now the back room was burning fiercely. The gunpowder would explode at any moment.

'Time to get out,' said Daco. 'Head for those trees. Let's go!'

Moving fast, Daco bundled Lankton out through the door and, followed by Mack, all three made for the trees at a crouching run, their clothes scorched and smoking. No one shot at them. They reached the trees and crashed through them for another ten, fifteen yards, heading for a rock big enough to shelter them from the blast. They squatted behind it, panting. Then a voice said:

'Well, look what the wind blew my way.'

Daco turned quickly and saw Dodds leaning on a rock not ten feet away. There was a gun in his hand. No prizes for guessing how he got there, thought Daco: being so familiar with the terrain, he'd know where men trapped in the cabin would be most likely to head for.

Lankton said:

'Dodds! Cut me loose and we'll finish off — '

''We' ain't going to do nothing, Tucker. I don't need you no more. You and me are finished.'

'But we got a deal! You said — '

'I lied. There's no 'we', there is no deal. First time we met, you tried to cheat me at cards. You didn't win then and you sure as hell ain't no winner now. I got all aces, six of 'em, in the chamber of my gun. So sweet dreams, Tucker.'

And barely taking aim he shot Lankton through the head. Tucker Lankton died not believing what was happening to him.

'A dead man don't talk. You two won't be saying much neither,' said Dodds and he raised his gun. 'The old man first, and then you, Daco.'

At that moment the mountain peace was shattered by a noise like a hundred locomotives crashing as the half keg of gunpowder exploded and sent burning debris high into the air. The blast blew Dodds off his perch and knocked his gun out of his hand and out of sight. But he recovered quickly, tried to retrieve the Colt which remained lost, then bunched his fists and leaped at Daco who was still getting to his feet. He looked dazed and there was blood running down one side of his head. Mack had been levelled by a falling tile or a spar of the roof and was well out of it. Daco felt for his gun, then remembered he'd given it to Mack.

As he straightened up, Dodds aimed

a round-house swing at him. If it had connected, it would have sent him to wherever Mack had gone. But still slightly off balance, Daco took a step back, thus converting a murderous knock-out punch into a glancing blow on the shoulder. The shock of it cleared his head and he put his fists up.

Dodds came on to him again. Daco kept him away with left jabs which snapped Dodds's head back. Dodds stood off and countered with accurate long-range punches with both hands which, if sustained, were the sort that cut an opponent's face to ribbons but don't put him down. Daco changed tack and targeted Dodds's body. Moving inside his guard, he landed a left to the heart and was rewarded by hearing a gasp of shock and pain.

This first flurry of punches taught each man respect for the other. Both were skilful fighters who were unlikely to take risks to get a quick victory. They would pace themselves, content to soften their man up until they saw an opportunity to put him on his back for good. They circled each other, looking for an opening. Daco thought he saw one, feinted with his left and aimed an uppercut which Dodds avoided and in return planted a sweet looping right on Daco's eye. He blinked with the power of it, shook his head and stuck his left jab back in his opponent's face. Dodds smiled grimly, hunched his shoulders and, with his chin tucked well in, advanced behind a flurry of short jabs.

Daco's right eye was cut and the blood blurred his vision. He wiped it away and bored into Dodds's body with a series of battering blows which brought his opponent's jaw down to meet the uppercut which landed low on the side of his jaw. But as he followed through, Dodds stepped to his left and caught Daco with a clubbing hook on the ear which rocked him to his heels.

But he kept moving, riding everything that Dodds threw at him; then, using his feet to move forward, he penetrated his opponent's defences, pushing him back with a succession of straight rights and short lefts. Dodds's face was puffy and a swelling the size of a hazelnut threatened to close his left eye. His breath was coming in great gasps and Daco sensed he'd got the measure of his man. Dodds was tiring fast, his punches grew wilder and they had lost their power. It was only a matter of time before his chin stopped one of Daco's deadly rights.

Daco had lined up his man and was about to turn Dodds's lights out when his opponent dropped his hands, stopped boxing, and lashed out with his right foot. But Daco saw it coming and grabbed the boot. He held it a moment, then gave it a mighty jerk. Dodds lost his balance and staggered back into the bushes. The hand he put out to break his fall found the butt of the gun he had lost. When he stood up it was in his hand.

'Back off, Daco.' He spat the words through swollen lips. 'I just changed the odds back to the way I like them. This is where the game ends. It's all come down to just you and me.'

'Why did you do it, Dodds? I mean all the lying and thieving and killing? You had a family, you had this place, lots of men would have been happy to make a life here.'

'Family!' Dodds snorted with contempt. 'Losers every one. Pa was a loser but at least he's dead. Ma is the kind of sweet little old lady I hate and Annie's a cripple. I'd never be free of them. I wanted to make something of myself. I had big ideas: it would be all or nothing.'

'You ain't going to get nothing,' said Mack who had come round.

Dodds was not expecting this. As he turned, Daco made a split-second decision to get away, fast, to draw Dodds after him. He didn't have a gun. It was the only way he had of protecting Mack.

As he ran, he heard Dodds crashing through the undergrowth as he gave chase. He risked a glance back but saw nothing. The explosion had set grass and shrubs and trees alight. He couldn't make Dodds out through the smoke, but this meant Dodds couldn't see him either. He whistled for Blackie who trotted to meet him. He swung up into the saddle and was a hundred yards away before Dodds stumbled out of the trees. He loosed off a couple of shots which went wide, then got his horse and set off in pursuit.

Daco had a short start which Blackie extended to a couple of minutes. He made for the mine, for he had half a plan. He dismounted, dropped his hat just by the mouth of the tunnel and scrambled up the valley to the rock he'd used as cover once before that day.

He was barely out of sight when Dodds arrived. He leapt off his horse, then stopped when he caught sight of Daco's hat which lay just by the pick and shovel he and Lankton had used and the half-empty box of gunpowder.

He smiled, eased his gun from its holster, cradled it in his right hand, then walked into the tunnel where all the signs told him Daco was hiding.

Once he was out of sight, Daco climbed down to the shaft. His plan was wild: to wrench out the first props that shored up the tunnel, cause the roof to cave in for a few yards and trap Dodds inside until he could get help to dig him out.

He reached for the pick and took a swing at the chock holding the first prop in place. His aim was true but the prop held. He swung again and the thud of metal on wood went reverberating into the darkness of the shaft. Daco heard a voice call his name. He struck again but the prop still refused to budge. A shot came from deep inside the tunnel. Daco raised the pick, not caring now if he made a noise loud enough to wake the dead, and dug the spike deep into the wood where it stuck fast and wouldn't be dislodged. There was no time to try again, for Dodds would soon be on him. Daco got out fast.

Dodds was coming out shooting.

One of the shots must have struck the keg of gunpowder. For just as Daco got clear, the shaft exploded in a cloud of choking dust. When it settled, the mouth of the tunnel had been sealed and all that remained on the side of the mountain was a scar of fresh earth. Daco lay on his back and looked up at the sky.

No man could have survived the blast.

This was not how he'd wanted it to end.

But it was over.

12

Silveroo No More!

'It's over,' said Daco to Mack.

Mack sat on a low wall that had survived the destruction of the cabin while Daco told him what had happened.

'I had me a look in his saddle-bag,' Daco said, rounding off his story, 'and found the rest of the money from the bank robbery. So that ties up all the loose ends.'

'Not all of them,' said Mack, 'there's two items outstanding.'

He said the fire that followed the blast had moved so quickly he had only just managed to save himself. Lankton's body had been in its path. There wasn't much left to bury, though he supposed they should take care of it, even a bad man didn't deserve to be left to rot. Daco agreed.

Then he added with an excited twinkle in his voice:

'I also got news that makes recovering my stolen goods small potatoes. Just take a look . . . '

Daco looked where Mack was pointing. He saw smoking timbers around the edges of a wide gash in the earth where the cabin had been.

'What am I supposed to be looking at?' he said, puzzled.

'Daco, you're a good friend but you don't know nothing about rocks. If you did but know it, you're staring at the igneous lying down with the sedimentary just the way the Good Book says the lion lies down with the lamb. This here is a *contact*! There's slate. That coarse-grained rock is granodiorite. And there's the quartz between the two of them. Best sandwich a man could ask for. 'Cos what you've got there, Daco, is a gold-bearing lode! Come on, I'll show you.'

With a hammer from his saddle-bag,

he began chipping at fresh-broken areas of the exposed rocks, breaking small quantities of quartz out of it until he had enough. He then placed the fragments in a pan and pounded them with an iron mortar.

Daco peered at the results but all he saw was crumbled rock and dirt.

'Here,' said Mack, 'carry on grinding up the rock. I want it pulverized as fine as you can get it. I'll go get water.'

By the time he came back with a bucket, Daco had reduced the quartz to a white powder.

'Good,' said Mack. 'Now pour some of the water on it, swirl the pan and sluice off the excess over the edge a little at a time.'

Daco added, swirled and sluiced away the powdered quartz.

'Now do it again . . . And again . . . More water . . . '

The water grew less milky until nearly all the quartz had been sluiced away, leaving only a small amount of sediment. Along the edge of this white residue was a line of some new material. It was yellow and it gleamed.

'I told you!' said Mack. 'We got *colour*!'

The yellow streak emerged more clearly as Daco went on sluicing until the last of the white quartz was gone and all that remained in the pan was a pinch of gold, as fine as snuff.

'I'd need my scales and to do some weighing before I could tell you how much to the ton it'll run, but it looks good. We'll also have to poke around in the little valleys and canyons hereabouts, where streams have cut through the bedrock, to get an idea of how far this contact goes.'

'Sounds like a long job,' said Daco.

Mack laughed: 'Hold your horses. There's no hurry. If there's gold, it's been here since before Adam met Eve and it sure ain't going anywhere. Besides, we're the only ones in the whole wide world that know there's yellow metal under this ground.'

'You're right,' said Daco with a smile.

'One thing bothers me,' said Mack.

'You told me old man Dodds was a geologist. So how didn't he spot the signs? He built his cabin right on top of a fortune. If I could find lodestone, he surely could have?'

'Maybe he never looked. Or maybe he saw all the signs and wasn't interested. A man must have a reason for hiding himself away up here. If he came to Silveroo from the town, maybe the gold he was after was something else, the simple life, answering to no man, being with his family, who knows?'

'That figures. But we also got to think how to handle this. In the ordinary way of things, I'd stake out a claim, the full acreage, and then ride back to Clayton to register it. Only I can't do that. This is private land. Belongs to Mrs Dodds and young Annie. All that's found here is theirs by law.'

'We'll have to tell them. Couldn't she give licences to someone who wants to work the gold? Take a percentage? Be no different from share-cropping.'

'I guess she could do that. But she'd

need help choosing the right man.'

Mack paused, then went on: 'But that ain't the worst problem. The toughest job is how we're going to tell Mrs Dodds that her darling Billy was not only a skunk of the lowest sort but that he died a bad man's death.'

'We won't tell her, nor Annie neither. We can't. We just say we met with Billy up here, back on one of those visits Mr Galt said he pays from time to time. We say it was Billy found the gold, that he died when a tunnel collapsed on him. Reckon she'd go for it?'

'I reckon she won't be too hard to convince, on account of wanting to believe the best of her Billy boy. He don't deserve it. But yup, I guess she'll accept it. And Annie too.'

As they rode back down the mountain towards Pocaloca in the gathering dusk, Daco said:

'Maybe Dodds does deserve some credit after all. If he hadn't tried to cheat the railroad company by salting that old mine, Silveroo would still be pretty worthless. But it turns out the gold is real, so the family will be rich twice over.'

'You're right. The railroad company will have to up its offer,' said Mack, 'and with what the mine brings in them ladies are going to be more than comfortable.'

Mrs Dodds wept when she heard that Billy was dead, but Annie, though upset, wasn't surprised. She said Billy had run wild, so it was just a matter of time before his luck ran out.

But when they learned that they were rich and that it was all Billy's doing, they took some comfort.

'I'll spend the money on doctors for Annie,' said Mrs Dodds. 'But first I'll order me those new curtains.'

They all laughed.

The women insisted on making supper for them. It was the least they could do.

Daco said he would be moving on, but Mack thought he would stay if they wanted him to. He and his partner, Ned

Thomson, would be glad to look after the business side of the Silveroo strike and work it too, if that was what the ladies wanted. Mrs Dodds, who knew nothing of business or mining but knew an honest man when she saw one, accepted.

After supper, Daco and Mack went down to Galt's stores to drink some whiskey.

'Drinks on you, Mack,' said Daco. 'You got your money back, you're flush! Me, I still got about ten of the fifty dollars pay Dodds left with Casey to give to me. It's a lot more than the seventy cents I had when I first set eyes on him and Lankton and Crants, so I guess I've come out of this ahead of the game!'

'Don't you concern yourself on that score,' said Mack, 'I'll see you don't go short. Barkeep!' he cried suddenly. 'Fill 'em up again. And make my friend's a large one. If ever a man earned it, it's Daco Ward!'

We do hope that you have enjoyed reading this large print book.

Did you know that all of our titles are available for purchase?

We publish a wide range of high quality large print books including:
Romances, Mysteries, Classics General Fiction *β β*
Non Fiction and Westerns

Special interest titles available in large print are:
The Little Oxford Dictionary Music Book, Song Book Hymn Book, Service Book

Also available from us courtesy of Oxford University Press:
Young Readers' Dictionary (large print edition) Young Readers' Thesaurus (large print edition)

For further information or a free brochure, please contact us at:
**Ulverscroft Large Print Books Ltd., The Green, Bradgate Road, Anstey, Leicester, LE7 7FU, England.
Tel:** (00 44) **0116 236 4325
Fax:** (00 44) **0116 234 0205**